The Pumpkin Pact

By

Charlie Dean

Cover design by
Charlie Dean

For all the lovers of autumn.

It's sweater weather!

Chapter 1

Andi drew back the heavy, flower-patterned curtains and welcomed in the first day of September with a huge smile. She loved autumn, and even though it wasn't technically here yet, the fact that it was now September meant the season of woolly jumpers, lace-up boots and spiced pumpkin lattes was almost upon her.

She threw open the bedroom window and took a huge breath of air, letting it fill her lungs completely and savouring it before taking a deep exhale. There was already a different vibe about the outside, a slight chill even, as if August had vanished, taking the summer with it. And wow, what a summer it was. Record high temperatures, sleepless muggy nights, and an electric bill through the roof to pay for the constant fans.

'Jesus, Andi, will you close the window.' The male form in the bed grumbled and pulled the duvet up over their head. 'It's bloody freezing.'

'I could get back into bed and warm you up?' she suggested, taking a step towards her boyfriend.

'It's too early for all that nonsense,' he declared and Andi knew he was already asleep because he was snoring again within a minute so she shrugged her shoulders and headed downstairs.

There was always some excuse, too early, too late, too hot, too tired, in fact she couldn't even remember the last time they'd had a cuddle, let alone sex. They were only in their mid-thirties, together for three years and here they were already not having sex. It hadn't always been this way; they couldn't get enough of each other. They had sex whenever they could. Luckily, they both had their own places as Drew was a bit of a prude and refused to have sex unless it was in a bed and now she thought about it, it was never particularly adventurous either, missionary or her on top was about it. Sometimes she just longed for him to come up behind her in the kitchen, pull her pants down and do it doggy style, bent over the counter. That, however, was not Drew's way.

In fact, she didn't know what Drew's way was these days.

She thought they'd at least be engaged by now but every time she broached the subject, he just mumbled something about how expensive it was to get married and why did she feel the need, they didn't even officially live together. He still had his belongings at the flat he shared with his mate, and only a bare minimum of toiletries and a few bits of clothing had appeared in her house over the years.

'Good morning, Pumpkin.' She walked into the living room and was instantly greeted by the wet nose and wagging tail of her husky Pumpkin, so named because he was orange with green eyes and she adopted him on Halloween, almost four years ago now. It turned out to be the best decision she'd ever made. He came everywhere with her, even to work at her family's farm shop. 'Have you been on the sofa again?' she scolded gently and was rewarded with a tongue lolling smile. The orange and cream tufts of fur left behind were clear evidence that he'd probably spent the entire night sprawled across the sofa rather than in his huge and very expensive bed.

Opening the back door to let him out, she popped a latte pod into the coffee machine and then took it outside and sat in the wooden arbour, listening to the birds singing their dawn chorus and watching Pumpkin chase a rather shocked pigeon away that had unexpectedly landed in the garden.

This was her idea of heaven. No one around, nowhere to be, just sitting and taking in the quietness of the morning with a warm cup of coffee and a soft blanket over your knees. Thursdays were always her day off, along with the occasional Sunday, Saturdays were a rarity, far too busy in the shop, so this was her day when she'd wave Drew off to work in his office and she'd curl up outside with a good book or on the sofa in front of the fire in the winter months.

'Where shall we go today, Pumpkin?' she asked as he bounded over. Another of her favourite things to do was bundle the dog up into the car and head out for a long walk in the countryside, just the two of them. Drew didn't do walks either. In fact, Drew didn't do many of the things that Andi enjoyed. She loved long walks, reading, weekends away, castles, horses, and dogs. Drew liked sitting in front of the TV binge watching series after series that were always full of violence. Andi liked fantasy and romance or good old-fashioned things like All Creatures Great and Small and Call the Midwife. Nice, gentle programmes. She was starting to realise that she didn't have much in common with Drew at all.

'How come you didn't wake me up?' Drew appeared at the kitchen door, yawning, and scratching his private parts under his pyjama bottoms. Andi hoped he'd wash his hands before touching the kettle and made a mental note to clean the kitchen once he'd left for work. 'Tea?'

'No thank you, just had one,' she raised her cup as if to prove this was true and shuddered as she heard him fill up the kettle, open cupboards and pour himself some cereal. Everything was now ready for a thorough cleaning. *How come you didn't wake me up?* She went over his words in her head. Hadn't she done just that and hadn't he complained? And since when had she become his alarm clock?

She scrolled through her phone for a bit and then when Drew went upstairs, she quickly wiped over the handles, sprayed the surfaces and made Pumpkin and herself scrambled eggs for breakfast. Hers was served on a freshly toasted English muffin whilst Pumpkin's was mixed with ham and placed in his Halloween bowl.

'I might be working late,' Drew yelled as he stepped out of the door, closing it before she could even respond okay.

'Come on, boy, let's go for a mooch.' They both headed up the stairs, Pumpkin jumping onto the bed immediately and walking round in circles three times before settling down. Andi pulled out her favourite burgundy jumper, putting it back straight away because it wasn't quite cold enough for that yet and settled on blue jeans and a burnt orange shirt with a pair of battered Vans that were on their last legs but were so comfy, especially on long hikes, that she just couldn't bear to part with them.

She felt wonderfully autumnal as she stepped out onto the drive, Pumpkin settled down on the back seat after having his harness clipped in and she drove a few miles to the nearby stately home where she'd been an annual pass holder for the past ten years.

The girl on reception welcomed her by name, fussed Pumpkin and exchanged a few pleasantries before Andi entered through the old wooden door, bowing her head as she did because olden day people were considerably shorter than her five-foot nine frame and then off along the gravel path.

The magnificent Georgian house stood off to the side, perfectly symmetrical from the front and like it belonged in Bridgerton. In fact, she sometimes imagined Anthony Bridgerton or the Duke of Hastings storming down the steps and whisking her away into the garden for a secret rendezvous. What wouldn't she give for a bit of romance right now? All she got was a polite, curt kiss goodnight these days.

'Come on boy.' She switched Pumpkin's lead with an extendable one. He wasn't a dog that could go off lead, his high prey drive meant he chased anything that moved and his speed and stamina meant he could cover a lot of ground in a very short distance, so unless he was in a secure field, he was always clipped on.

Andi strolled towards the river that ran through the grounds of the house, imagining days gone by with girls in posh dresses being escorted for a scenic trip around the gardens, parasols up on hot days to shield their skin from the sun or a fan to be used seductively over their bosoms. Why were they usually referred to as bosoms back then?

There was a beautifully and intricately carved stone wall near the river's edge and an exquisite veranda that led down to steps which Andi knew many a maiden would have taken a gallant hand and stepped elegantly into a waiting boat. With her luck she'd have ended up tripping on her gown and falling headfirst into the water. She'd never have been one of those petite and gentile ladies. She was big busted, big bummed and taller than the typical male so picturing herself in Georgian attire was quite hard, yet their dress style did flatter the fuller figure, with the way it flowed from under the bust and skimmed the middle region.

Drew nicknamed her a Heffalump, and until recently she'd thought it quite endearing, a pet name if you will but when she'd unintentionally let it slip to her friend Chloe she'd been appalled and now she recognised it was a subtle way of criticizing her weight without being overly obvious about it.

'I don't know why you stay with him,' Chloe had continued as they'd enjoyed cocktails in the town centre one Saturday night, Drew had gone into Birmingham with his mates. 'He does nothing for you, treats you like shit and yet you still stay with him. If he was good in bed, I could maybe understand but you said even that's a bit lack lustre.'

Lack lustre wasn't the word. On the rare occasions when they did have sex these days, he would just start playing with her boobs a little, maybe a few kisses and then hopped inside and before you could say Bob's your uncle, Fanny's your aunt, he'd be done. She didn't even get a cuddle after, just the rhythmic sound of his snoring which usually meant she'd get up and sleep in the spare room.

'How have you done that?' Andi looked down at Pumpkin who had somehow managed to tie his lead around a tree and try as she might he couldn't understand what *No, the other way,* actually meant and was getting more and more tangled up. 'Stay there,' she instructed as she held his collar and unclipped his lead and then tried to thread the lead back on itself at the same time as holding on to a wriggling thirty kilo husky.

In hindsight, Andi wasn't sure if it was the squirrel or Pumpkin that was more surprised when it suddenly fell out of the tree a few feet from the dog's nose. Both of them froze, staring at each other and Andi watched in horror as the squirrel ran off, Pumpkin hot on its heels.

'Pumpkin!' She left the lead where it was and chased straight after him but a husky in full flight is not an easy catch and she soon had a stitch. 'That bloody dog!' She ran as fast as she could, pinching her side to ease the pain when she heard a voice from nowhere.

'Have you lost a dog?' The male voice called.

'Yes,' she called back, relieved and walked towards the voice.

As she rounded the bend, she saw what could only be described as an extremely wet Lord Bridgerton, emerging out of the river.

Chapter 2

The man was saturated from head to toe, clad in a white shirt that stuck to his chest and had become entirely see through, brown britches that left little to the imagination and he even wore riding boots that came up to his knees. He was carrying a somewhat damp Pumpkin who was currently licking his face. Although the man looked well built, the weight of a wet husky was causing some issues and as soon as Andi had clipped the other lead on, he placed Pumpkin gently on the ground and took a deep breath.

'I am so sorry.' Andi quickly apologised. 'His other lead got tangled and then there was this squirrel.'

'It's ok,' he motioned with his hand as if recusing dogs from rivers was an everyday occurrence for him. 'I didn't realise he'd be quite as heavy as he was.' The man bent down to ruffle Pumpkin's ears who took advantage of the chance to give himself a good shake, spraying more water on the man and Andi.

'It's his fur you see.' Pumpkin was on the longer haired side of a husky as Andi's house and hoover could tell you. She'd gone through three vacuum cleaners since having him because despite a weekly groom and a six-monthly de-shed, he moulted almost constantly.

'I just saw him leap in when the squirrel jumped up into that tree.' He wiped the fresh beads of water from his face with one hand and smoothed his dark hair back with the other, replacing his hands on his hips. 'Thought he might get in a bit of trouble.'

'Very kind of you.' Andi didn't think that it was the right moment to tell him that she'd taken Pumpkin for swimming lessons and that he regularly swam in this very river, albeit on his lead.

'He's a handsome devil I'll give you that.' The man knelt and began talking to Pumpkin who resumed licking his face. Andi had never been so envious of a dog in her whole life, not that she wanted to lick this man's face or anything but from this angle she had a very good view of his torso. 'Always wanted a dog but I'm never at home enough.' She was picking up a slight Yorkshire accent. 'Always at work.'

'Pumpkin comes with me,' Andi responded, beaming from ear to ear and trying desperately not to look at his amazingly toned thighs through the sodden material of his trousers. 'My family owns a farm shop not too far from here.'

'Cute name.' He stood up again. 'Suits him.'

'I adopted him on Halloween you see.' She was longing to ask why he was dressed in clothes from two hundred years ago but didn't really know how to broach the subject. 'Can I buy you a drink? Least I can do.'

'There you are, Andrew.' A woman dressed in tailored trousers and a shirt, carrying a clipboard and with a headset on came up behind them. 'We've been looking all over for you.' She spoke into the microphone. 'It's ok, I've found him.' She returned her attention to the man whom Andi guessed was named Andrew. 'You're needed on set,' she spoke, took a long look at him, and then shook her head. 'We're not doing the river scene yet, Jesus!' She stormed off speaking into her headphones. 'We're going to have to delay, Andrew needs a full costume change, makeup and hair.'

'Looks like you're in trouble,' Andi looked at him apologetically. 'I really am sorry.'

'It's okay,' he shrugged. 'I have to change all the bloody time anyway.'

'Are you shooting a film or something?' Andi looked at him again. 'Are you a famous actor?'

'The fact that you have to ask means I'm clearly not,' he laughed. 'I'm just doing a favour for my friend Kim. That was her just now. Bit of a battle axe but a good egg. She's an amateur filmmaker and apparently, I have the right look to play a Georgian Lord.'

'I have to say I agree with her.' Andi looked him up and down. 'Very Bridgerton.'

'I'm no Jonathan Bailey.' Andi was impressed that he knew who the actor was.

'Oh, I don't know; I think you'd give him a good run for his money.' What the hell was wrong with her? Flirting with a stranger in broad daylight whilst in a relationship. She'd be so angry if she found out Drew was doing something like this.

'Perhaps you could be my Viscountess?' he looked at her, one eyebrow slightly raised, and Andi thought she was imagining the sexual tension that had suddenly built up between them. 'I'm Andrew by the way but you can call me Andy.' He held out a hand. 'Although you probably guessed that from Kim.'

'Andi,' she took his hand, laughing.

'It's customary, I believe, that when a gentleman introduces himself, a lady responds with her own name.' She laughed again.

'I did, I'm Andi, with an i.'

'I'm so sorry.' They were still holding hands. 'Perhaps I can be Drew instead?'

'Oh God, no!' she said far too quickly.

'Do we not like Drew?' His hand was soft but slightly rough on the fingers, like he used his hands on a regular basis.

'It's my boyfriend's name.' Shit! Why had she said that? He dropped her hand almost instantly and his demeanour changed just as quickly.

'Well, it's been lovely to meet you both.' He gave Pumpkin another quick stroke. 'But I'd best be getting back, or Kim will have my guts for garters.' And with that, he turned his back and walked off towards the house. Andi could have literally kicked herself.

What the hell did you say that for? she chastised herself repeatedly as she headed back to retrieve Pumpkin's lead, carefully swapping it for the shorter one lest he see another squirrel.

The rest of their walk was uneventful, but she did catch a glimpse of the actors and crew as she walked out again. She went to raise a hand to Andrew but then remembered he'd probably be filming, so she just put her head down and went back to the car.

The sudden thunderstorm that afternoon did nothing to lift Andi's melancholy mood. Usually she loved a good storm and would watch from the back bedroom as the lightning streaked across the sky and the thunder rolled overhead but today, she just sat on the sofa with a bottle of red wine and watched her go to movie, Sweet Home Alabama. Pumpkin wasn't a fan of storms, so he was huddled next to her on the sofa, one eye opening slightly every time there was a clap of thunder.

This was how Drew found them at seven o' clock that night.

'Bloody hell, Andi, you look a right sight.' He picked up the empty bottle and glass and took them into the kitchen. 'Is this all you do on your days off?' he said, after coming back in. 'Pumpkin! Off.' The dog growled at him a little but immediately did as he was told and curled up instantly on the floor instead. 'Cover yourself up will you, your stomach's hanging over the top of your jeans.'

Andi pulled her top down; the wine had only made her feel worse and now Drew's berating was making her feel twice as worthless as she usually felt lately. What on earth had happened to her? She used to be so full of life and energy, but nowadays she liked nothing more than spending time on her own, even nights out with Chloe were few and far between.

But what grated her the most at this very moment was the look in Andrew's eyes, the look of disgust that she could be flirting with him when all the time she had a boyfriend. And really, what else did she expect? Decent men didn't flirt with other people's girlfriends, and decent girlfriends didn't flirt with other men.

'Have you had a good day?' Feeling guilty, she tried to pull herself together and slapped a smile on her face. 'Have you eaten? Perhaps we could order a takeaway?'

'Our new client took us out for a late lunch, so I'm just going to grab a sandwich.' This was becoming a regular occurrence, eating at work. They barely ate at the same time anymore, barely went to bed at the same time, rarely hung out together unless it was something to do with family and they were expected to be there as a couple.

'I'll just make some pasta or something then.' She walked into the kitchen, opened the back door, and smelled the air, that wonderful smell of rain on hot earth, petrichor was it? She recalled a Doctor Who episode years ago where she had first heard the word.

She couldn't be bothered to make a sauce for the pasta and there weren't any ready-made ones in the cupboard, so she grated some cheese on it once it was done and melted it under the grill, just what she needed, comfort food. Oozing hot cheese that dangled out of your mouth.

'Bloody hell, that stinks,' Drew said, getting up off the sofa as she sat down next to him, holding his nose and being generally over dramatic.

'It's only a bit of cheddar,' Andi remarked, digging her fork into the bowl, and swirling the spaghetti around. 'I've had it many times before.'

'It's never smelt like that before.' He sat down in the chair on the opposite side of the room and Andi curled her feet underneath her, Pumpkin asleep on the floor beside her. 'Watch what you're doing with the sofa, will you, it will be all bent out of shape with you sitting like that.'

Andi was getting a bit annoyed now. 'It's my bloody sofa Drew, I'll sit on it how I like.'

'That's how we're playing it, is it?' Without warning, he stood up and started unplugging the TV. 'Well, I pay for this with the Sky, so I'll take it upstairs and watch it in the spare room.' He walked towards the door that led upstairs.

'Bloody hell, Drew, what's got into you?' she asked. 'I've just had some pasta and cheese and sat on the sofa the same way I've always sat on the sofa.'

'I'm just pissed off with work.' He put the TV back on its stand. 'I shouldn't take it out on you I know, but it looks like I've been passed over for promotion yet again. Five years I've been at that place, five bloody years and I'm still only a junior consultant. Jack was made partner last month, and he started nine months after me.'

Perhaps it's your shitty attitude? she longed to say but instead said, 'Maybe you could chat to Mike about it, he always seems easy to talk to at the Christmas parties.'

'Mike's gone,' he tutted. 'Some bloody woman in charge now called Sapphire. I mean, who calls their child Sapphire?' he scoffed, plugging the TV back in with a heavy hand.

'You didn't tell me that.' Andi finished off the last of the pasta and passed a bit of cheese to Pumpkin, who had woken up when he realised that there was the slightest possibility of this actually happening.

'Didn't I?' he seemed genuinely perplexed. 'It's been months, loads of upheaval. Are you sure I haven't mentioned it?'

Andi shook her head. 'I'm positive I'd have remembered if you had. Didn't Mike have a leaving party or anything?'

'No, all very hush, hush.' Drew switched on the TV, immediately flicking onto Netflix. 'A bit suspect if you ask me, lots of rumours and Chinese whispers.'

'What kind of rumours?' But that was all the information she could get out of him because he'd already retreated into his latest show and there was no talking to him when he did this. Andi quickly washed up, grabbed her book and blanket and sat outside under the fairy-lit gazebo until it was too dark to read.

Chapter 3

'Morning Dad, morning Mum,' Andi called as she walked into The Pumpkin Patch the next morning at exactly seven thirty. She had got this down to a fine art. She was never early and never late but always bang on.

'Cutting it fine, as always,' her dad remarked.

'Actually, Dad, I'm bang on time,' she smiled at him. 'As always.' She headed out the back, Pumpkin already making himself at home in his allotted space, safely behind a closed door in case of attempted escapes. Andi often wondered why he always tried to run off, he was fed, walked, and spoilt rotten on a daily basis, most dogs would be more than happy with that but maybe it was a husky thing or just a Pumpkin thing, this need to seek adventure all the time. Andi couldn't say she blamed him.

'Tea.' Her mum handed her a cup and so began the daily ritual. Sweep out the shop, mop the floor, stack the shelves, and order deliveries. The monotony of it all sometimes gave Andi a headache, but she wouldn't swap it for the world. She spent nearly every day with her parents, got to meet new people who had never been to the shop before and got to chat with the regular customers.

The Pumpkin Patch had been her dad's idea a few years ago. He'd been made redundant from the car factory he'd worked at since he was sixteen, had no idea what he was going to do.

He could have retired on the money he was given as a pay-out, but instead he announced over family Sunday dinner that he'd bought a shop.

Andi had been flabbergasted, her mum irate and her brother just laughed, but when they all went to visit the shop, rundown that it was at the time, the passion in her dad's voice made them all share his vision and they all agreed to help as much as they could. Her younger brother, Lewis, only did the odd shift, but his wife Fran was on the permanent rota along with Preeti and Kane, the two-part timers.

The Pumpkin Patch had originally been a shop attached to an old farm, but as farming declined, so had the shop and although the farm carried on, the shop was closed and sold on along with some fields. With Andi's family buying it, it became an all-round produce shop, and the farmer was delighted.

They sold fresh milk and cheese from the dairy cows at the farm, vegetables from other local farmers and locally sourced products, such as homemade jams and cakes. It had taken a while, but the shop was really coming into its own and they were even thinking of expanding at some point.

'I can't believe how well we did on ice cream this year,' Andi commented as she pulled out yet another empty carton from the freezer. 'The hot weather has really helped.'

'It's been a wonderful summer,' her mum agreed. 'And there's definitely been an increase in tourists this year, I just wish we weren't so far off the beaten track.' Andi noticed a little slump in her mum's body language.

'We're doing ok though?' she asked.

'Costs are going up and I do worry about having to raise prices to match, but it would be nice to do something else, something a bit different, draw more people in rather than just the ones that drive by and see the sign.' Andi took her mum's hand reassuringly.

'Don't you worry, Mrs Wilson,' she said lovingly. 'Your clever daughter will think of something.'

'How are you anyway?' Her mum changed the subject as they stacked the newly delivered marrows. Stacking marrows was a very hard job, they are not in the slightest bit a regular shape and the Wilsons prided themselves on taking all vegetables, wonky or not so quite often the task of making the produce look neatly packed was an impossible one. 'Drew still being an arse?'

It always made Andi laugh to hear her mum swear. Kathy Wilson had grown up in a strict catholic household and barely used bad language, but now and again if she was really pissed off it flowed like a fishwife on the docks.

'I've found out what's been bothering him.' She always felt better after talking to her mum. 'There's a new boss at work and he thinks he'll get passed over for promotion again.'

'Maybe he could try being a bit nicer then.' Andi looked at her over the carrots. 'I'm sorry Andi, I know you love him, goodness knows why, but he can be a right arrogant twat.'

'MUM!' Andi almost dropped the tomatoes she was trying to balance.

'What's the matter?' Andi's dad looked over from the honey pots.

'Mum just called Drew an arrogant twat.' Andi couldn't believe she was having this conversation.

'But he is though, isn't he, Dennis?' Kathy looked to her husband who walked over to her.

'I'm afraid I have to agree with your mother on this one.' He placed an arm around his wife's shoulders. 'He does nothing for you, Andi. If I thought he loved you and treated you kindly, well, I'd forgive his narcissistic traits, but when was the last time he took you out for the day or gave you flowers?' She knew her parents were right, but it still stung.

'Or had sex?' Kathy blurted out.

'No, Mum,' Andi shook her head; this was a step too far.

'You're always saying how prudish he is. Sex is part and parcel of being in a healthy, mature relationship,' Dennis butted in, much to Andi's horror. 'Why, just yesterday your mum and I did it on the hay bales out the back.'

'Oh God!' Andi put a hand to her mouth. 'Too much information.'

'Now who's being a prude?' Kathy giggled as Dennis ran a tender hand over her backside.

'Stop it!' Andi screamed. 'I'm not being a prude; I just don't want to know about my parents and their…' She couldn't even say the word. 'Sexual habits.'

'Who's got sexual habits?' Preeti, their sixty-five-year-old employee, walked in.

'My parents.' Andi walked over to Preeti, hoping for an ally. 'They shouldn't be doing it at their age.'

'Why the bloody hell not?' Preeti asked. 'That's why I'm a bit late if I'm honest with you. Owen was feeling a bit randy this morning and the pipes were working shall we say so we made the most of it,' she winked at Andi.

'Jesus Christ!' She walked out into the back. 'You're all sex mad,' she shouted before tripping over the hay bales and grimacing in disgust.

Andi wasn't a prude, far from it, but the thought of her parents having sex at their age and Preeti and Owen, well, it just did something funny to your insides. She'd never thought about the older generation having sex, but she supposed they must do, after all, did desire suddenly go away just because you hit fifty? She doubted it. The thought of her and Drew at fifty made her sad all of a sudden so she grabbed Pumpkin's lead and took him out for a wander.

The fields always helped clear her head, there was something about nature and the outdoors that gave you the space to think and make decisions and she knew she had a very important decision to make and soon.

She wanted to marry and have children at some point and the clock was ticking on the latter of those two. Women were waiting longer and longer these days to start a family, but it was also riskier the older you got, and did she really want to be sixty with a twenty-year-old? No, she had to sit down with Drew and have a good talk with him about what he wanted for the future, how did he see them as a couple, that kind of thing. She heard Chloe's voice in her head.

But it doesn't matter what he wants, it's always about what he wants, what do you want, Andi?

That was the problem, she didn't really know what she wanted. All these years she'd longed for a tall, dark, and handsome stranger to fall at her feet. Romanced and cherished and return the favour. To love your partner as much as they loved you, like her parents did. She wanted to be someone's everything, that they couldn't live without but with Drew, she didn't even think she was his anything.

Gilbert Blythe in Anne of Green Gables had a lot to answer for. She'd watched a TV adaptation with her mum when she was a teenager and fell in love with him. He loved Anne, unquestionably, with all her faults and her temper and although she didn't know it at the time, Anne loved him back. A meeting of equals, a couple that lived for each other, that wanted the other to be happy even above their own happiness.

So why are you with Drew then?

A question that she had often asked herself. Was she scared to be on her own maybe? Surely not. She'd been on her own for most of her twenties and quite enjoyed her own company. She didn't need a man in her life to make her feel complete, but she wanted one.

But the wrong one is worse than none at all.

Andi wasn't sure why the little voice sounded like Chloe, it was probably because it was the kind of thing she would say, in fact, she had said it on numerous occasions after her string of disastrous relationships, finally leading her to Miley after admitting to everyone that she was in fact gay. Andi had known, of course; Chloe had confided in her when they were fifteen that she thought she fancied girls. However, she never had the courage to do anything about it until Miley started working at her office.

So what are you going to do about it? Stay with Drew and be miserable or tell him to fuck off and have a chance of happiness on your own or with someone new?

'What shall I do, eh, boy?' she asked Pumpkin, who was currently sniffing around. She checked her watch, realised it was almost opening time and headed back towards the shop to walk down the long drive and open the gate. That was her and Pumpkin's job when they were in.

The drive wasn't a drive as such, it was a rather rough dirt track with the odd pothole, and due to yesterday's rain, these potholes were now large muddy puddles that Pumpkin thoroughly enjoyed splashing in.

'I'm not rescuing him again if he falls in.' A familiar voice called, and Andi's head shot up to see Andrew walking up the road.

What on earth was he doing here? she asked herself.

'I hope you don't mind; the gate wasn't open, so I just jumped over.' He was almost in front of her now. 'I was just on my way to work when I saw the sign and thought that maybe this was the farm shop you mentioned yesterd…a…y…' The last word trailed off in a small scream as Pumpkin, in his excitement to see his would-be rescuer, bounded over to him, ran round his legs, causing the lead to tangle and Andrew quite literally fell at Andi's feet.

Chapter 4

Unfortunately, right at Andi's feet was an exceptionally large and deep pothole, which had previously been filled with water but was now filled with a wet and muddy Andrew and the rest of the contents were splashed up Andi's jeans, even reaching her jumper. Pumpkin was completely oblivious to the accident he had just caused and was instead, standing on Andrew's back with his front paws, with the sole intent of trying to lick his face once again.

'I'm so sorry.' Andi was immediately apologetic and did her best to help Andrew to his feet, not an easy task with Pumpkin bounding about and a lead wrapped around his ankles. What on earth must this man think of her? Clearly, she shouldn't be in charge of a dog.

'Do you think he's trying to kill me?' Luckily, Andrew laughed as he spoke and helped Andi detangle the lead and the dog from his legs. 'Or just get me wet all the time?'

'He succeeded in drenching me too.' Andi looked at her clothes, she was going to have to go home and change before serving in the shop or maybe she could hide out in the back all day and wear one of the long aprons.

'It's only on your bottom half though, I'm covered.' Andi was glad of the excuse to look him up and down and surmised that he was indeed covered from shoulder to toe in muddy water, only his face seemed to have escaped but at the expense of his hands and arms where he'd instinctively put them out in front as he fell.

'We can get you cleaned up in the staff toilets, I'll just open the gate.' The gate was only a few yards away, but Andrew walked with her, Pumpkin trotting along in the middle of them. He never did that, Andi noted to herself. All the way back to the shop, he walked right at heel, almost unheard of, he was usually bouncing about in front, sniffing everything in sight.

'Oh my word.' Kathy exclaimed at the sight of them as they walked into the shop. 'What happened?'

'Pumpkin happened.' That was all Andi needed to say.

'Well, we've all been there,' Dennis declared. 'Come on, Son, I'll show you where you can get cleaned up.' He ushered Andrew through the back of the shop, trying hard not to touch him.

'He's not going to be coming back again anytime soon, is he?' Kathy said, fetching the mop and bucket back out and angrily scrubbing at the floor where Andrew had dripped muddy water. 'Grab the wet floor sign, would you, Andi.' Andi did as she was told. 'We can't lose customers before they've even stepped inside the shop.'

'It's okay, Mum,' she reassured, placing the yellow sign by the door. 'He's a…' What was he exactly? A friend? She couldn't call him that, she'd only met him the once, well, twice now and what exactly was he doing here? From what he'd said, he meant to come here, maybe not the first thought when he woke up this morning but when he saw the sign, he hoped it was where she worked. She couldn't help it, but her heart skipped a little at the thought.

'He's a what, dear?' Preeti asked, faffing with the till roll.

'Actually, I'm not really sure what he is.' Andi told them quickly what had happened the day before and both of the older women smiled knowingly at each other.

'He likes you,' Kathy announced.

'Don't be daft, Mum,' Andi replied. 'The look he gave me yesterday was nothing short of hatred.'

'That's what men do though isn't it, play hard to get,' Preeti declared. 'It's all about the chase these days.'

'It doesn't matter anyway, whether he likes me or not,' Andi proclaimed. 'I'm with Drew and I'm not looking for another relationship.'

'The toilet's free if you need to clean yourself up.' She hadn't realised that Andrew was now standing right behind her and had heard this last statement but if he was upset by it, he didn't show it.

'Thanks, I'll just wash my hands.' Andi almost ran into the toilet. 'Idiot!' she shouted at herself in the mirror. 'That's twice now you've mentioned a boyfriend in front of him and he hasn't even shown any interest in you other than rescuing your dog.' Andi washed her hands, took her jumper off, luckily, she was wearing a t-shirt underneath and grabbed her dad's Pumpkin Patch jacket hanging up outside. Her dad was even taller than she was, so it covered a good portion of her dirty jeans, but she'd definitely have to stay out the back or behind the till if a customer was about.

She arrived back in the shop to the sounds of laughter, and Andrew regaling them with yesterday's tale about Pumpkin. Even though Andi knew her mum and Preeti had already heard it, they chuckled as if it was the first time.

'Straight out of Pride and Prejudice,' Andrew continued. 'Except Mr Darcy wasn't rescuing a dog.'

'Pumpkin's a bugger for water,' Dennis said. 'He's always swimming in that river. Whenever we go, come rain or shine, he leaps in and has a good paddle.'

Andrew went quiet and looked at him. 'He can swim?' Everyone nodded as he burst into laughter himself. 'Well, that'll teach me.'

'Did you get the scenes finished?' Andi asked, desperate to keep the conversation away from anything to do with what he'd just heard her say.

'We did,' he nodded. 'There's still loads more to do because we all work, so it's only evenings and weekends that we can get together to shoot.'

'Andrew's friend Kim is an amateur filmmaker,' she told the other three. 'She's shooting a Regency piece at the Abbey.'

'That's exciting. Does she need any extras?' Preeti asked. 'I've always fancied myself as a saucy wench.' She pushed her overly ample bust up with her hands and Andi looked away mortified. Luckily Andrew just laughed.

'I'll let her know you're available,' he said and then looked at his watch. 'I'd best be off to work.' He started to walk towards the door.

'What is it you do?' Dennis asked.

'Landscape gardener,' he replied. 'I just love the outdoors, always have, ever since I was a kid.' Dennis and Kathy exchanged a look.

'You're not too bothered about being dirty then,' Preeti laughed at her own innuendo.

'No,' he shook his head. 'I'm usually a lot worse than this, but I was on my way to quote for a job, but it doesn't matter,' he shrugged his shoulders. 'I've got a jacket in my van so the worst will be covered up.

'Take a couple of sausage rolls with you, the least we can do.' Kathy hastily wrapped two of the freshly baked rolls in a paper bag. Andi shook her head gently. It was such a motherly thing, making sure people were fed. When she was younger, it was always her house her friends came to during the school holidays because they knew Mrs Wilson would have freshly made bread or cakes going and cold cans of pop. 'I made them myself this morning,' she smiled proudly. 'Award winning they are.'

'By award winning, she means they came first in the county show last summer.'

'Still award winning,' her mum said.

'Thank you,' Andrew smiled as Kathy pressed the bag into his hands. 'I'll enjoy these with a cup of tea later on.'

'Make sure you come back again soon,' Dennis rushed to open the door for him.

'I definitely will.' Andrew looked at Andi as he said this and after feeling her mum's hand on her back, pushing her forward so hard that she almost slammed into him, she declared that she would walk him to the gate. 'That would be lovely. But you'd best leave Pumpkin this time. I'm not sure I could cope with any more water today.'

'I really am sorry again for Pumpkin today.' Andi wasn't sure what else to say. 'And for yesterday.'

He stopped walking and turned to her. 'It was yesterday that I wanted to speak to you about actually.'

'Really?' They started walking again, moving to the side as a car drove past, beeping its horn, the occupant waving at them. 'That's Mrs Bradshaw.' She told him. 'Every Friday, regular as clockwork.'

'You have lots of regulars, do you?' Andi nodded.

'Most of our customers are regulars,' she sighed. 'Mum would love us to be busier, we're not struggling or anything, the business ticks over nicely and keeps us all in jobs but it would be nice to have something else to focus on, some outside trade perhaps, not just people that drive by and see the sign.' She laughed when she realised that was exactly what he'd done.

'About yesterday.' They had reached the gate, now open with a cattle grid, although this wasn't strictly necessary as the farm animals were kept securely in fields on the other side and he rested his hands on the top bar.

'Sorry I didn't say Pumpkin could swim; you got all wet for no reason.' He shook his head.

'That's not what I'm trying to say.' He looked up at the sky as if it would give him courage. 'I was rude to you.'

'You weren't rude to me,' she placed a hand on his. 'You were gallant and kind.'

'No, afterwards.' He didn't move his hand and she didn't move hers. 'I was rude to you when you said you had a boyfriend.'

'Were you?' She dismissed it. 'I didn't notice,' she lied.

'Yes, you did. I saw it in your face.' He placed his other hand on top of hers as he turned his whole body to face her. 'I don't think I imagined it, but we had a connection and when you said you had a boyfriend, it reminded me that I had a girlfriend and that I shouldn't be flirting with another woman, I'm not that kind of a bloke. I've never done that before in my entire life, but there was just something about you that made me completely forget about Carla and then when you said about Drew, I felt so guilty that I stormed off.'

'Oh.' She took her hand gently and rather reluctantly from the middle of his.

'I get the feeling you don't particularly like Drew though?' His hands fell to his sides.

'It's not that exactly. I love him and all that, but it's just...' Why was she telling this stranger?

'It's just with me too.' The way he was looking at her right now was just as Mr Darcy looked at Elizabeth over the ballroom floor. As if all he wanted to do was whisk her away and make love to her, but he had to hold himself back with every ounce of strength. 'I'd best be going.'

'Will you come back?' Andi asked. She didn't know what else to say.

'I don't think that would be a very good idea.' He walked behind her, brushing her hand lightly as he passed. 'For either of us.'

Andi didn't say another word, just nodded quietly and watched him walk out on to the road and get into his van that was parked up just outside the gate. She'd never felt so wretched in her whole life. It took her a good ten minutes to find the strength to move from the gate and even then; it was only because Mrs Bradshaw beeped her horn again on the way back down that dragged her out of her little stupor.

'Wasn't he a lovely young man?' Kathy said to her as she walked back into the shop.

'Handsome bugger too,' Preeti agreed. 'If I were thirty years younger.'

'It wouldn't matter if you were thirty years younger.' Andi snapped. 'He's got a girlfriend; I've got a boyfriend, and that's all there is to it.' She stormed into the back and spent the rest of the day angrily rearranging stock, counting deliveries and making orders. At the end of the day, she grabbed Pumpkin, said a curt goodbye, and headed home.

Thankfully Drew was once again working late, so she sat outside and cried.

Chapter 5

True to his word, Andrew didn't come back, and she found herself moping about like a thirteen-year-old with a high school crush. Drew had somehow pissed her off even more than was usual and instead of her normal apologetic behaviour she snapped at him, which sent him into a mood and now they hadn't spoken for three days.

Monday morning, however, Drew was already up and dressed and waiting for her in the kitchen. She saw his abnormally happy face and became suspicious.

'Amazing news.' She was usually a morning person, but today she just wasn't feeling it. 'I'm on the shortlist for the promotion.' He opened his phone. 'Woke up to the email this morning.' He shoved the screen under her face and took it away again before she'd even had a chance to read the subject line.

'That's great news, Drew.' She forced a smile but didn't think he'd notice either way. 'I'm really pleased for you.'

'It does mean I've got to go to London for the night though.' It was at this sentence that Andi noticed a small suitcase by the front door.

'You're already packed.' Andi found this a little suspect since he'd only received the email that morning and had barely anything at her house anyway. 'Is that my suitcase?'

'You don't mind if I borrow it do you?' she shrugged. 'I haven't got time to go to the flat, so I've just popped the few bits in from here, we're all booked on the nine o' clock train to Euston.' He downed the last of his tea and threw the cup in the sink. A notification on his phone lit up. 'That's my Uber.' And he was gone out the door. 'See you tomorrow.'

'Bye then,' she said to the empty hallway as Pumpkin waltzed in from the garden. 'Fancy a woodland walk this morning?' she asked him, feeling lighter than she'd felt for a long while. The shop was always closed on a Monday, due to being open the rest of the week. It was the only way her parents would take a day off together. Even if Andi, Lewis, and Fran were there, at least one if not both of her parents would be in at some point. 'Shall we treat ourselves to breakfast out?'

Her usual morning jolliness returned as she quickly showered and dressed, got Pumpkin in the car, and headed out to one of her favourite places in the whole world.

Books and Brews was a dog friendly bookshop and café, although shop was a wholly inadequate term. Department store was probably better. Housed in converted barns, the books stretched across three floors with second hand and new ones, a whole barn dedicated to children and young adults with a story telling tree in the middle. The café served the best breakfast for miles and even had a doggie menu too.

'Hello, Andi,' Claire, the owner, called as they walked in. She came around the counter and went straight over to Pumpkin to make a fuss of him. 'I've had loads of fantasy books in since your last visit.' Claire knew exactly the books that Andi liked to read and that's what made it such a special place.

'I can't wait to have a look.' Andi was excited. 'But first we need feeding.'

Claire laughed. 'Go on through, we're not busy, only one other customer so far, so Harry will be glad of the orders.'

Andi walked down to the end of the barn where the café was. The aroma of bacon and fresh coffee merging with the smell of old books made her feel like she was in heaven. They went straight up to the counter and ordered a full English for Andi and sausage and eggs for Pumpkin. Harry gave her a bowl of water for Pumpkin and as she walked over to her favourite table by the window, he suddenly jumped up, causing her to spill its entire contents over the gentleman that was sitting reading a newspaper.

Andi gasped. 'I am so sorry.' What was it lately with Pumpkin and water? 'He's usually so well behaved.'

'I'm inclined to disagree with you on that.' The man put down his paper, but Andi already knew who it was by the voice. 'We really should stop meeting like this.' She could tell from the huge grin on his face that he was pleased to see her and she knew she was beaming with joy as well.

'Andrew!' He was the very last person she expected to see but if she was being honest with herself, he was the only one she wanted to see.

'Why is it that on the three occasions that I've met you and this unruly husky.' He laughed as he said the last bit. 'I always seem to end up wet.'

Andi couldn't help it, first she tittered, then she giggled, and then she burst into uncontrollable laughter and Andrew joined in. 'I really am sorry.' She pulled a packet of tissues out of her bag, and he took them gratefully, taking a few out and dabbing at his face and hair.

'At least I'm not soaked through this time.' He joined in with her laughter.

'I should go.' She went to step away. 'It was nice to see you.'

He placed a hand gently on her arm to stop her. 'Join me.' She shook her head, even though she wanted to. 'Please.' She didn't know if it was the way he looked at her as he said it or the way he said it, almost like a lover's caress, but she nodded, placed the now empty bowl on the floor and sat opposite him at the table.

'I've never seen you here before,' Andi said as Pumpkin sat waiting eagerly for his breakfast. She noted there was an empty plate and cup in front of Andrew.

'I could say the same about you,' he replied as Harry came over with a plate for Andi and a bowl for Pumpkin.

'I've let it cool on the windowsill,' Harry said, placing it on the floor next to the husky, who demolished it in seconds and then returned to remove the bowl and bring back his water. Pumpkin lapped it up and then lay down under the table and promptly fell asleep.

'Do you come here a lot then?' Andi asked, placing her egg on her fried bread so it caught the yolk.

'When I can,' he paused for a minute. 'I haven't stopped thinking about you,' he spoke quietly, even though there was no one else in the room. 'It's been maddening. I almost drove to the shop yesterday. I feel like a lovesick teenager. Carla wanted to know why I wasn't eating.'

'Drew and I had an argument; we haven't spoken all weekend.' There she was again, spilling her secrets to a stranger, but he didn't feel like a stranger, he felt like a kindred spirit. 'I just don't know what it is with him, he's started working late, permanently on about promotions, never seems happy and we just don't do anything together anymore.'

'It's the same with Carla,' Andrew agreed. 'She's got no interest in anything outside of her job, says she has to work twice as hard as the men to prove herself, she hasn't had a day off in four months except for Sundays. Mind you, we don't really have much in common, now I think about it. She likes foreign holidays in the sun but give me a windswept walk on the moors any day.'

'You're from Yorkshire, aren't you?' She'd almost finished her breakfast.

'When I was little,' he nodded. 'Not much of an accent left now. Haven't been back for a while.'

'I went to York once with my parents.' She mopped up the last bit of egg with a piece of bacon. 'Absolutely fell in love with the place.'

'Yorkshire is a bit bigger than just York,' he said. 'But I'll agree with you, it's a lovely city.'

'Always wanted to go back there, but never got round to it and Drew doesn't do this country.' She put her knife and fork down on the plate. 'God, I'm stuffed.'

'It sounds like Drew and Carla are cut from the same cloth.' He looked at his phone as a notification came in.

'Perhaps they should be together instead of with us.' Andi cringed at her words. 'Sorry, didn't mean that.'

'Do you think we're attracted to each other because we're unhappy?' Andi was gobsmacked. 'There's no point beating around the bush, say it like it is I reckon. I like you, Andi and I'm pretty sure you like me, but we're both in relationships and you seem like a decent enough girl that doesn't go around cheating on her boyfriend and I certainly have never cheated on my girlfriend and haven't even thought about another woman until I saw you the other day.' He stopped suddenly. 'Tell me if I've overstepped the mark.'

'No, no, carry on.' She gave him the permission to continue, eager to know what he had to say.

'So I kind of got to thinking about what had changed, why do I have this irresistible pull towards you? And all I could come up with was that I was unhappy.' He fanned his hands out in a helpless gesture. 'Trust me, that took a lot to admit it to myself. I love Carla, I really do, but lately it just doesn't seem to be working. She seems happy though so I kind of think it must be me.'

'I feel the same,' Andi admitted. 'Drew seems his normal self except for the work stuff and it's natural after a few years for the passion to die off, isn't it?'

'Is it though?' Andrew asked. 'If I'm being honest, I'd have sex far more than we do currently, but it's like she rations it, as if it's a hold she has over me and I only get it if I've been a good boy.' He looked at Andi in amazement. 'I honestly can't believe I've just said that.'

'I can't believe you've just said it either.' Harry came over to the table as Andi spoke, and she was grateful of the interruption into her thoughts and the envious feeling of Andrew having sex with another woman.

'Refills?' They both nodded as he poured more coffee into their cups and cleared away the plates.

'You're just so easy to talk to.' He poured three packets of sugar into his cup, followed by some milk. 'I could have chatted with you for hours on Thursday and Friday if I hadn't had somewhere else to be.'

'Are you free now?' What was she doing?

'Yes,' he said simply.

They spent the next few hours together, milling through the bookshelves, picking out books and enjoying an afternoon tea in the café. Before they knew it, the whole day had flown by, and they were both the proud owners of many new books.

'I can't believe I didn't recognise your van.' Andi was standing by her car, Andrew's van next to hers.

'It's not very memorable, it's just a plain old van,' he said, patting the roof. 'I've had a really good day.'

'And me, I can't remember the last time I laughed so much,' she replied, bending down to click Pumpkin into his safety harness. 'I really need to get back and feed him though, he gets antsy if he goes much past five.' Andi was reluctant to get in the car and Andrew seemed the same, but she could think of no reason to linger.

'I'm closing the car park now,' Claire said, as she came out of the barn door, locking it behind her.

'We'd best go,' Andrew concluded. 'Like I said, I've had a really good day.' And with that, he got into his van and drove off, waving out of the window before disappearing out of sight. It was with a heavy heart that Andi drove home, she had no idea when she'd see him again, had no way of contacting him which was probably a good thing given the fact that she was having naughty thoughts about him constantly. What had got into her? She was turning into some sex starved nymphomaniac, judging by the visions of her and Andrew making love in all sorts of random places.

She woke up the next morning drenched in sweat and breathing heavily from a rather vivid dream involving hay bales, so she jumped straight into the shower before work, grabbing a McDonald's breakfast for everyone on the way.

Although she hadn't known when she would next see Andrew, what she really hadn't expected was him turning up, halfway through the morning shift.

'Have you got a minute?' he asked, popping his head round the door. She looked to her mum, who nodded eagerly and so she met him outside. 'I've had an idea how we can both help each other.'

Chapter 6

'What are you talking about?' Andi asked, not following what he was saying at all. 'An idea for what, exactly?'

'Walk with me,' he said, and she nodded as he led the way along the back of the shop and out to the pumpkin field. 'Does this belong to you?'

'We rent these fields from the farm, but the shop and the land to the side are ours,' she answered proudly. Row after row of pumpkins stretched as far as the eye could see. 'It will soon be harvesting time.'

'And you just pick them up and put them in the shop?' he enquired, and she nodded. 'Might have another idea.' He seemed to drift off into a world of his own.

'How about you tell me what the first idea is and then we'll go from there.' Andi was desperate to know what he was going on about.

'So…' he began, pausing, Andi thought it was for dramatic effect and was about to throttle him when he spoke again. 'You love your boyfriend but don't think he pays you enough attention, I have the same problem with my girlfriend, so I was thinking…'

'Go on,' Andi encouraged.

'How about we make a pact to make them jealous?' He looked at her as if he'd said something earth-shattering.

'That's it?' Andi wasn't impressed. 'That's the big idea.'

'Hear me out.' He stepped backwards onto the gate and sat on the top; Andi did the same. 'What's a sure-fire way of getting our respective halves to show some interest?'

'I could run round this field naked, and Drew probably wouldn't bat an eyelid.' Andrew's eyebrows raised seductively at this point.

'Enough of that,' he coughed, changing the subject. 'If they thought there was someone else on the scene, it might just give them the kick up the arse, they need to realise what lovely partners they have and start treating us a little better.'

'But there isn't anyone else on the scene,' Andi declared. 'And even if there was, I'd never cheat on Drew.'

'What am I?' Andrew asked. 'Scotch mist?'

'Are you suggesting we have an affair to make our other halves jealous?' Andi had to pretend to be outraged, because even though she'd never do it, the thought of rolling round in the pumpkin patch with this handsome man was considerably appealing right now and doing the most insane things to her insides.

'Not have an affair, no, of course not,' he said, jumping down and standing in front of her, one arm either side of her, resting on the gate. 'But just start name dropping, especially good for you with me having the same name as your boyfriend, that will really infuriate him.'

'Even if we did, and I'm not saying we do.' Andi couldn't believe she was even contemplating the idea. It sounded utterly absurd. 'How can I start dropping your name into conversations? Drew knows everyone that works here, and I don't go anywhere else on a regular basis to meet new people.'

'Well that's where the other idea comes into play.' He was looking up at her so intensely and with such an honest and open expression on his face that she thought, if she just leant down a little bit, she could place a kiss on those soft, delicious lips. *Stop it.* She told her brain. 'I have to admit, I hadn't fully worked out how it could work but when you showed me this.' He turned and swept his arms around. 'Tik Tok.'

'Okay, you've totally lost me now,' she shook her head at him.

He grasped one of her hands in his and ignored the bolt of electricity that shot up her arm. 'Follow me.' He led her along the rows of pumpkins. 'What's the hottest thing right now?'

'In what respect?' She really didn't have a clue.

'You have heard about Tik Tok haven't you?' she nodded.

'I've never been on it though,' she admitted. 'Isn't it just like Facebook and Instagram reels?'

'Yes and no.' He pulled out his phone and showed her a few examples. 'Look at this.' He clicked on a video showing scores of people queueing for a chip shop. 'This one is just down the road, the owners made a silly jingle, it went viral and now people drive for miles, a group of lads came all the way from Scotland.'

'All because of a video on Tik Tok?' Andi scoffed. 'Don't be daft.'

'It's true.' He showed her a few more. 'This chap just comments on people filling up jars and things then 'has a moment' and this lady trials lots of gadgets. Look how many followers they have.' Andi couldn't believe it. 'And this lady pretends to be Draco Malfoy because someone told her she looks like him, she is funny though.'

'Are you suggesting we should do something like that?' Andrew nodded.

'You've got a gorgeous little shop, beautiful fields and a dog,' he said. 'People go mad for a dog.'

'But what would we do?' Andi realised that they were still holding hands and dropped his like it was a hot potato.

'Dogs cooking goes down well, mock ups of films, one chap pretends to be Mr Darcy.' He looked sad when she let go of his hand, but Andi noticed he recovered himself quickly.

'I don't know, Andrew, I'm not very creative.' She couldn't even write a poem about Christmas when she was at school.

'Leave that to me and I'm sure Kim would help,' he suggested, but she still wasn't sure. 'Listen.' He must have sensed her hesitation. 'Have a think on all of it, we can say we're working together, all innocent and above board and technically we would be working together so we're not lying or anything.'

'I'll think about it.'

And think about it she did, all that evening while Drew
watched the latest season of Cobra Kai, she sat in the garden
with Pumpkin and waded through Tik Tok videos.
Somehow, three hours had passed by, and it was time for
bed. She had particularly enjoyed the dog ones, as Andrew
had said she would, and she found it bizarre how quickly the
time had gone.

Drew had fallen asleep on the sofa, the TV was still playing
so she switched it off, said goodnight to Pumpkin quietly
who had obediently gone on his bed and tip-toed up the
stairs, so she didn't wake Drew. The thought of having the
bed to herself for another night and not having to put up with
his snoring sounded like heaven and she crawled into the bed
covers, spread out like a starfish, and fell asleep almost
immediately.

Her dreams were filled with random things which, when she
thought about them the next morning, she knew had come
from the videos. But the constant appearance of Andrew and
a rather dirty vision involving a bed of pumpkins made her
wake up in a hot, sweaty mess.

'You ok?' Drew asked, standing in the doorway. 'You were
calling my name and moaning.'

'Was I?' She was relieved that the light was off, and he
couldn't see her blushing.

'Well, you used my full name, which is a bit strange, but
then that's dreams for you.' Andi had never been more

thankful in her life that Drew was officially Andrew. 'Unless you've got some new secret man I should know about?' Andrew was right then, she thought. All she'd done was say a man's name in her sleep and he was already sounding jealous.

'Don't be silly,' she said, pulling back the covers. 'Come in and keep me warm.' And to her surprise, he did just that, cuddling up to her and kissing her neck. She was astonished to find that he was already aroused, and they made love for the first time in months. She didn't climax, she never had with Drew, but it was nice to feel close to him all the same and for once, he didn't just roll over and go to sleep.

'What do you think then?' Andrew had arrived at the shop the following Friday morning before they'd even opened and Pumpkin had greeted him so enthusiastically that he knocked him into one of the displays, causing Andrew to cut his hand and now Andi was administering some first aid.

'I'm not sure,' Andi said. The past few days with Drew had been lovely. He was still coming home from work late and falling asleep on the sofa, but every night since his return from London, he'd climbed in beside her and woken her gently to make love to her. She'd even almost climaxed last night. She was so close she could almost touch it but just as she was about to burst, Drew moved slightly, and the rhythm was lost.

'What aren't you sure about, love?' Kathy asked, clearly eavesdropping.

'Tik Tok videos,' Andrew announced. 'I thought we could look into doing some promo ones for the shop.'

'That's a brilliant idea,' Dennis agreed, appearing suspiciously out of nowhere. 'Your mum practically wets herself at Hayley Morris and that Stage Door Johnny is hilarious.'

'Hayley Morris?' Andi vaguely remembered watching one of hers. 'The lady that dresses up and acts as body parts?'

'That's the one,' Kathy laughed. 'When she checks into the vagina hotel as her period, just brilliant.' Andi didn't know whether she was more astonished at her parents watching Tik Tok videos or the actual content of what they were watching, but she was certainly learning a few things about them lately.

'What did you have in mind?' Dennis asked, greeting the farmer, who'd just come in with a fresh supply of cheese and butter from the dairy and a new batch of honey from their beehives. 'Oh, I love a bit of honey on my waffles.'

'I'm not sure yet.' Andrew pressed the plaster to his arm that Andi had just placed there. 'Did you say waffles?' he asked, and Dennis nodded.

'I did,' Dennis said, baffled. 'Kathy makes them fresh on a Monday morning.'

'That's it!' Andrew leapt up and kissed Dennis on the lips. 'It's genius, Dennis, inspired.' He pulled out his phone and started tapping at his screen, it looked to Andi as if he were messaging someone. 'Kim can be here this afternoon if you fancy it. Can you get the rest of the staff in at all? It would be great to have as many different faces as possible, but maybe not all on screen together.' He headed out of the door. 'I'll be back later with some props, and we'll run through it a few times after closing,' he said as he went out of the door.

'What is he babbling on about?' Kathy asked. 'Did you give him some drugs or something?' She looked at Andi.

'Of course not, Mum.' She followed him outside, almost having to run to catch him because he was walking so fast that he'd virtually reached the gate. 'Andrew!' She called. 'Will you slow down and tell me what on earth you're going on about?'

He turned round at her voice, a huge smile on his lips. 'Waffles,' he said simply.

'Waffles,' she repeated. 'What about waffles?'

'It's going to be fantastic,' he grabbed her shoulders. 'First of many, combine harvester, strawberry fields and oh my word…' He trailed off. 'Lady Marmalade will be awesome.'

'Andrew!' She put her hands on his cheeks and made him look at her. His eyes were bright with excitement. 'What will be awesome?'

'Songs with food in the title.' He answered.

'I still don't get it.' Was she being thick?

'You know the song, Waffle House?' Andi nodded. 'We do a spoof version of it using stuff from the shop. You must have seen it on Tik Tok? Where you sing the chorus and then the band pop up?' Andi nodded at the vague memory. 'Then we've got Strawberry Fields Forever, strawberries. That Combine Harvester one, out in the fields. See?'

'Okay, but what do you mean by we?' She was sure she knew the answer already.

'All the staff, that's what will make it funny,' he assured her. 'Anyone can have some young people doing it but using the staff in their uniform is what makes it unique. The Pickle Grove Pumpkin Patch will be an internet sensation.'

'But you said Lady Marmalade too.' Andrew nodded. 'I am not dressing up in stockings and suspenders for the world to see.' She was horrified.

'Well if you won't, I'm sure your parents will.' And Andi had a suspiciously sinking feeling that Andrew was correct.

Chapter 7

'Do you know what would work really well?' Kim and Andrew were discussing various things that evening. Andi, Dennis, Kathy, Preeti, and Kane had jumped at the chance of being involved, but they'd been unable to get hold of Lewis and Fran so they'd decided they could shoot theirs later on. 'Popping up from behind the shelves.'

'And the till, and through the door even,' Andrew suggested, and Kim nodded.

It was now an hour after closing and everyone but Andi was enthusiastic and raring to go. She was desperate to get home. Drew said he was going to be on time, and she'd wanted to cook them a nice meal. She'd even picked out some sexy underwear to greet him at the door with. Nothing too obvious, just a nice corset with stockings and suspenders. She'd thought she'd wrap her dressing gown round her first and then once he was in the door, she'd let it fall open for the big reveal. Then he'd whisk her upstairs and make love to her or maybe they wouldn't even reach the stairs, maybe he'd be so consumed with passion that he'd carry her into the living room, and they'd do it on the sofa.

There was only one problem with this thought, when Andi envisioned it in her head, it was Andrew that she saw. Andrew's face lowering his lips to hers, Andrew's hands caressing her breasts, Andrew's voice moaning her name as she ran her hands down his chest and further into his jeans, opening up the zip and…

'Andi!' Her dad's voice interrupting her thoughts jolted her, and she realised her mouth was open and she shut it with a snap.

'What?' She couldn't help the blush that spread across her cheeks as her gaze wandered towards Andrew who was currently positioning everyone.

'We're ready for a take,' Dennis said.

'Oh right, okay.' She hadn't a clue what she was meant to be doing and where she was meant to be standing so Andrew ushered her into position, placing some cucumbers in her hands. 'But why aren't we using waffles?' she asked.

'For the hundredth time,' Kim scolded. 'We're promoting your shop, your goods, you don't sell waffles so what would be the point of using them?' Andi still didn't understand but nodded anyway.

It took many takes, shouts of exasperation from Kim and goodness knows how many bursts of laughter, trips, and falls, in fact they had more scenes for a blooper reel rather than for a full video, but Andrew was over the moon with it all.

'I'll come back tomorrow and shoot some stuff with Pumpkin out in the field, I've had a brilliant idea for him.' It was dark outside by the time they all walked into the car park. Long summer evenings felt like a thing of the past and the nights were drawing in quick and fast now.

'I haven't enjoyed myself so much for a long time.' Preeti announced as she got into the car with Kane who always gave her a lift home. Kathy and Dennis only lived a few minutes away, so they had started walking down the drive to lock the gate after everyone. Kim had long since left and Andrew and Andi stood by their respective vehicles, Pumpkin on his lead was having a quick sniff about before Andi clicked him into the car.

Andrew was leaning on the bonnet of his van, looking out at the fields. 'It's really beautiful here, isn't it?' he asked, looking over at her as she closed the door on the car and walked over to him.

'I've always loved it.' They stood staring at the night sky; a few stars were just beginning to shine, and the moon was peeking out slightly from behind a cloud. 'It's definitely better than being cooped up in an office all the time. I don't know how Drew does it.' She wished she hadn't mentioned Drew because she felt Andrew stiffen.

'You seem happier today,' he said.

'Do I?' Was it that obvious? Did her happiness really rely on Drew paying more attention to her? It was a sobering thought.

'I've been thinking,' he started. 'My idea about making our other halves jealous was a bit silly.' Andi looked at him. 'We'll still do the Tik Tok things, I really enjoyed it, but I think we'll forget our little pact.'

'Why?' Andi sat on the bonnet next to him. 'I think it will work, with a few ground rules.'

'Are you two going to stand there all day?' Dennis had walked back up the drive. 'Some of us have got homes to go to you know.'

'Sorry, Dad.' Andi bid Andrew goodnight as her dad tutted, got in her car, and drove off.

The house was in total darkness when she got home, she checked her phone in case she'd missed a call or a text from Drew but there was nothing. It was almost nine, where could he be? She hadn't realised how hungry she was, so she fixed herself a quick piece of toast and a cup of tea, Pumpkin had been fed at the shop, so he was given his dental treat as she sat down in the living room.

She didn't know whether to text him or not, didn't want to seem like a possessive girlfriend but then on the other hand what if he'd had an accident. What if he was laying injured somewhere, bleeding or maybe even dead. Don't be silly, she told herself, his drive home was an easy one, all main roads so even if he'd had an accident, he'd be found, and someone would have rung her.

But by midnight he still wasn't home, there was no answer when she rang so she fired off a text to say she was worried and could he ring her as soon as possible. Maybe he'd gone back to the flat and just forgotten to tell her, yes, that will be it, she thought.

Of course she didn't sleep, how could she? Even having Pumpkin on the bed beside her did nothing and at four, she gave up, came downstairs, and made a cup of tea. She checked the news and local Facebook forums, but there was nothing suggesting any accidents. What had happened to him?

She must have eventually dozed off because the next thing she knew, she woke up to a knock on the door.

'Where have you been?' She threw her arms round Drew as he stood there, relief clear in her voice.

'I'm so sorry,' he hugged her. 'We went to the pub after work, had a few too many, and I ended up on Jack's floor. Didn't realise until later that I've left my phone and key at work, so I won't be able to get it till Monday. I woke up this morning and realised you'd be frantic, so I called a taxi and came straight here.'

'I was worried sick, Drew.' The relief she had first felt turned to anger as she heard that he wasn't hurt or injured but just passed out on his work colleague's floor after drinking too much and hadn't had a thought for her sitting at home all this time. She turned and stomped up the stairs.

'Don't be like that, Andi.' He followed her up, standing outside the bathroom after she had slammed the door almost in his face.

'I need to get ready for work,' she shouted. 'Some of us have been up all night and now need to do a full day on no sleep.'

'I've said I'm sorry.' She could tell he was getting annoyed with her tantrum now and usually she would subside and give in, but she had had enough of that over the years. He'd had no care for her at all, not even messaging her to say he was going out. What if she had got dressed up and cooked that special meal like she wanted to, what a fool she'd feel, even more of an idiot than she felt now.

'Why don't I cook us dinner tonight?' Andi's ears piqued; Drew had never offered to cook dinner. 'I'll pop out and grab us something nice and it'll be ready for when you get home. Maybe we could sit and watch a film?'

She opened the door and looked at him, he appeared sincere. 'That would be lovely.' She wouldn't hold her breath though and didn't intend getting her hopes up, he'd disappointed her enough over the years, but maybe, just maybe he was changing and starting to realise, as Andrew had said, that she was indeed a lovely girlfriend.

When she arrived at work, her heart skipped a little when she saw Andrew already there waiting for her. He was standing by the counter, her mum hovering around him like a bee to a flower. He was in his usual work attire; jeans and a t-shirt and her dad was talking to him about something, Dennis looked up as she came in and gave her a reproachful look.

'Sorry I'm late, I overslept.' Was all she said, she wasn't about to give them another reason to hate on Drew, they really didn't need anymore.

'Can I take Pumpkin?' Andrew asked.

'He probably won't go with you,' Andi remarked. 'I know he likes you, but he usually only walks with people he really knows.' Pumpkin proved her wrong by sitting at Andrew's feet. 'Or not.' She handed the end of the lead to him.

'We'll only be in the pumpkin field. Come and join us in a bit but give me a few minutes to get sorted.' He whisked Pumpkin out of the door, the dog didn't even give Andi a backward glance.

'That's loyalty for you,' Andi scoffed.

'He's just a good judge of character.' Kathy said and Andi knew this was a dig at Drew. Pumpkin didn't particularly like Drew and certainly would never let him walk him on his own, not that he'd even tried.

'I'll put the kettle on, shall I?' Andi walked out the back in an effort to avoid further comments about Drew, subtle or not. She really wasn't in the mood. She was knackered from her lack of sleep and feeling irritable and snappy. Grabbing the notebook from the drawer in the small office that they used for writing delivery orders in, she took out a pen, sat in the chair, and started writing a few ground rules. Things like no kissing, holding hands etc…silly things really, and she didn't know why she was doing it.

As if Andrew was going to be trying to seduce her and her him. They both had other halves, and both had stated that they wouldn't ever cheat on them. It was a business deal, nothing else, but the silly rules were making her laugh now and she finished off by naming it The Pumpkin Pact and then just folding it up and placing it in her work fleece pocket.

After a cup of tea, she headed outside to the fields and found Pumpkin sitting perfectly still, wearing a black jacket whilst sitting in the middle of some fairly decent sized pumpkins and numerous toy cars. The pumpkins were also wearing jackets in all sorts of colours.

'Like it?' Andrew handed her the lead. 'Stand as far from him as you can, maybe lie down so I can try and hide the lead in the photo.

'Is there a reason for the cars? And the jackets?' she asked, doing exactly as he said but kneeling on the floor, she wasn't about to lie in the mud.

'From the video, where they're dancing in and around the cars.' Andrew took a few shots, then walked over to her and showed her them. 'See, the pumpkins are the people.'

'It's a dog and some pumpkins in clothes.' Andi wasn't impressed.

'Just you wait,' he said, taking a photo of Andi. 'You're going to be pleasantly surprised.'

And surprised she was.

Chapter 8

'Now, it's only rough,' Andrew warned, setting up his laptop in the storeroom the following day. Everyone gathered around as the opening sounds of Waffle House blared out.

'That's brilliant,' Kathy declared as the video showed Andi and Preeti popping up from behind the till a number of times with various different vegetables.

'Look at Pumpkin.' Dennis pointed at the screen, at the part where Andrew had somehow got the cars to look life size against the dog and pumpkins.

'Honestly Andrew, that's amazing,' Andi declared.

'It is good, isn't it?' Andrew nodded, almost to himself. 'I need to cut it down a bit as it's far too long and Tik Tok videos aren't overly long, but I think a minute should be enough to get the message across.'

'Have you told Carla you're working with us?' Andi asked Andrew after her parents had gone back in the shop and Andrew started packing his laptop away. Pumpkin was busy sleeping in the corner, as was his usual and most favourite hobby.

'I've started dropping a few hints,' he replied, zipping up his bag. 'I'm still not sure it's a good idea though to be honest. It feels a bit devious if I think about it.'

'You can't back out now,' Andi said rather quickly then realised this had come across as rude. 'I mean, it's just, Mum and Dad are so excited about the Tik Tok videos, I'd hate to disappoint them by saying you won't be doing them anymore.'

'Oh no, I wouldn't do that,' he said. 'I've really enjoyed being here and working with you.' Andi thought he had finished the sentence, but instead he hurriedly said. 'All! Working with you all, I meant.'

'That's good to know,' Andi smiled at him. 'It's already working with Drew, by the way. He's already far more attentive than before and I've only mentioned your name once or twice.' She didn't tell Andrew that the first time had been in her sleep whilst dreaming about him kissing her all over whilst covered in pumpkin spice latte.

'I'm glad.' He didn't sound glad, Andi thought, if anything he sounded disappointed. 'Carla just seemed happy I was going to be out of the house more when I mentioned coming here.'

'Really?' Andi hadn't liked Carla from the first moment Andrew had mentioned her, but she was disliking her even more because she was causing him to be sad and she didn't know why she felt so strongly about it, but she really didn't like the thought of Andrew being sad. It made her heart feel heavy in her chest.

'I think I annoy her,' he said simply.

'How could you annoy her?' Andi asked. 'You're funny and kind, sweet and generous. Why would anyone find that annoying?'

'I think I might be too nice,' he shrugged his shoulders.

'Too nice!' Andi was in disbelief. 'How can anyone be too nice?' she asked. 'Give me a guy who treats me nice over an arsehole any day. Too nice indeed. Don't you go bloody changing a thing or you'll have me to answer to. Too nice, I'll give her too nice. Some people don't know when they've got a good thing.' She trailed off then, realising that she'd been speaking out loud and rather vehemently.

'Thank you,' he laughed gently. 'That means a lot.' Their gazes locked for a moment and Andi felt the sudden urge to place a hand on his face and caress his cheek. He looked so sad behind the eyes, like the weight of the world was on his shoulders and she longed to kiss his troubles away.

'Yes, well' she stumbled over her words, reining her thoughts in before they ran away from her. 'Carla is a very lucky woman.'

'And Drew is a very lucky man.' Andrew picked up his case, said goodbye to Pumpkin, who barely lifted his head and then walked through the shop saying farewell.

If only he knew. Andi said to herself, and she wasn't sure if she meant Andrew or Drew.

'I thought we could go out for a roast,' Drew suggested as Andi returned home to find him all dressed up, freshly shaven and smelling gorgeous. All she wanted to do was veg in front of the TV, but the enthusiastic look on his face made her dash upstairs and jump into the shower. When she came back down, she found that Pumpkin had been fed, his bowls were washed up and Drew was waiting for her with a glass of wine in his hand. 'I'll drive.' This was almost unheard of. Andi always drove. Drew liked to drink more than she did, not that she didn't enjoy a few glasses, but it was definitely more of a thing for Drew.

The home cooked meal the previous evening hadn't materialised, instead Drew had ordered a Chinese takeaway and they had sat and watched The Hit List, shouting out the names of the songs from their introductions and then downloaded the new Indiana Jones film. When Andi returned from making a cup of tea for them both, she saw Drew scrolling through Tik Tok and thought it would be a good time to mention Andrew.

Drew had bristled instantly at the other man's name, which made Andi smile on the inside.

'I could have helped you with that.' He had suggested and Andi knew she'd hit a nerve when he offered it.

'You're far too busy with work.' She had said. 'You get that promotion sorted.' Then she had stroked his thigh and he'd virtually pounced on her. They almost made love on the sofa, but Drew got a little put off when Pumpkin decided to see what they were doing and growled at him.

'Shall we try The Stag and Pheasant.' Drew asked as they got into his car, and he started backing off the drive.

'But that's miles away,' Andi complained. Now that food had been mentioned, her stomach was rumbling.

'We'll be there in no time,' he said. 'Jack said it's really good. And apparently the puddings are to die for.' Drew knew her well; puddings were her downfall and the reason she would never be a svelte size twelve.

'You know how I feel about pudding.' Andi sat back in the seat of the car, which felt a little further forward than normal, perhaps it was just her imagination, but she reached below and pulled it back a couple of slots. That was better, her long legs felt much more comfortable.

'Yes, I know how you feel about pudding.' Was she reading into the way he glanced at her stomach or the disparaging tone with which he stated it?

She decided to brush it off. 'I've definitely got a pudding stomach,' she replied and thought she heard him tut but really couldn't be sure. 'Andrew showed us the video today, it's really good, Mum and Dad are so excited about it.'

'You'll have queues out of the door before you know it,' he said, paying attention to the tricky junction at the crossroads near their house. 'What's the next step in the great Pumpkin Patch Tik Tok empire?'

The drive to the pub was uneventful, but it took longer than Andi had expected. They chatted some of the way about future videos before the conversation inevitably turned to Drew's work.

'So when will you know if you've got the promotion?' she asked as they finally pulled up in the pub car park. It was already quite full, and she hoped they'd be able to get a table fast as she was ravenous, and her legs were aching after being cooped up in the car for so long. She didn't relish standing at a bar for ages while they waited.

'Middle of October,' Drew replied as he took her hand in his and led her inside. Andi had to admit that the pub was gorgeous. It had an old -fashioned and homely feel to it whilst also being modern and bright. She finally understood why so many people raved about it on Facebook. Her mouth was watering just from the aroma of roast beef.

'Have you made a reservation?' The young girl asked as they stopped by the wooden podium.

'I'm afraid not,' Drew answered, and the girl shook her head. Andi's heart sank as she watched her scour the list in front of her and then turn and gaze around. 'I might be able to squeeze you in around eight?'

'That's two hours away,' Andi complained to Drew. 'Let's just go to The Elms.'

'We're here now,' he said, squeezing her hand a little too hard. 'We'll take it, thank you,' he said to the girl and gave her his name. She wrote it down and then showed them the way to the bar.

'Drew?' Andi and Drew both turned to face the female voice. 'I thought it was you.' A woman had stood up and was approaching them. 'Have you got a table?' She asked as she reached up to kiss him on both cheeks, even in four-inch heels, she was much shorter than him.

'Sapphire.' He returned the kisses. 'What on earth are you doing here?' Andi noticed that she held onto his arm slightly longer than was necessary. She racked her brain, Sapphire? Boss Sapphire? 'This is my girlfriend, Andi,' he introduced her. 'Andi, this is the new managing director, Sapphire.'

'It's so lovely to meet you.' Andi felt like a giant in comparison to this petite woman. As they shook hands, no kisses for Andi she noted. She felt like she would break under the pressure.

'Likewise. Drew has told me so much about you.' Andi wasn't sure whether this was true or not. 'Did they manage to find you a table? We had to wait nearly an hour and we'd already booked.'

'Got a two-hour wait,' Drew complained. 'We'll just sit at the bar and have a few drinks.'

'Nonsense.' Sapphire tapped his arm with her elegantly manicured hand. 'Come and sit with us, I insist.'

'We couldn't impose.' Andi didn't want to go and sit with strangers. She'd come out for a nice dinner with her boyfriend. 'The management won't be happy with us doing that either, it will be like skipping the queue.'

'Just come and sit with us while you wait then.' She clearly wasn't taking no for an answer, Andi reasoned and without any protest from Drew, they found themselves seated at a table for eight. Drew was sandwiched between Sapphire and another woman and Andi was placed rather unceremoniously on the end, as far away from Drew as was possible, it would seem.

Andi had no idea who anyone was, but clearly Drew obviously did and the entire table prattled on about business and sales. The gentleman sitting near Andi asked what she did for a living and when she replied that she worked in her family's shop he looked at her as if she were something he'd just stepped in, and no one bothered talking to her again.

Her mind wandered to Andrew and her pact with him, well, at this moment it was still a very one-sided deal, could she even exploit him like that if he didn't agree to it? Was it right to do so? Would he be mad at her if he found out? But how would he find out? It wasn't like they were best buddies, once he'd filmed a few videos he'd be off, never to be seen again. This thought filled Andi with such sadness that she almost felt like crying.

She looked over at Drew. No, he was her priority. Let's make him jealous and maybe then he'll propose. He caught her gaze as he leaned in closer to Sapphire and murmured something in her ear that made her laugh and tap him playfully. He raised an eyebrow at Andi and lifted his glass to her. She smiled back. *Looks like he's playing a little jealousy card all of his own, well, two can play that game.*

Chapter 9

'I think you should meet Drew.' Andi blurted out the next day at the book café. She'd arranged to meet Andrew there to have one last look at the video before creating an official account and publishing it.

'I don't want to meet Drew,' Andrew said, sounding shocked that she had even suggested such a thing. 'Why would I want to meet him?'

'We have to up the stakes.' She cut through her piece of treacle tart rather angrily and some of it flew off the plate, landing right in front of an eagerly awaiting Pumpkin.

'We need to what now?' Andrew turned off his laptop. 'I thought we agreed not to do it.'

'It was your bloody idea in the first place.' Andi was becoming agitated. The entirety of Sunday evening had been sat watching Drew and Sapphire fawn all over each other, taking any and every opportunity to touch each other or be close. When Andi had confronted him in the car about it, he had merely shrugged and remarked, 'See, you don't like it when the shoe is on the other foot.' And she had taken this to mean her recent comments about Andrew.

'And now I've decided it was a stupid idea.' He took hold of one of her hands as she went to stab the tart again. 'You may as well give it all to Pumpkin right now and save yourself the time and energy, because if you carry on like that, it will be on the floor anyway.'

'Sorry.' She cast a glance at him from across the table. His eyes were so kind, filled with a tenderness she hadn't seen in anybody else except maybe her dad. 'It's all fucked up.' Andi placed her head on the table and knocked it gently a couple of times. 'I'm such an idiot.'

'Hey.' With his other hand he raised her head. 'You are not an idiot in the slightest,' he reassured her. 'You've just got an arsehole for a boyfriend.' Andi had no idea how he'd made this assumption, which was correct but still an assumption nonetheless, when she'd only told him a few things. 'Your mum told me he can be downright nasty to you.'

A light bulb went off in Andi's head at this. 'Been chatting with Mum, have we?'

'They don't really like him, do they?' he said.

'They never really have, if I'm honest with you,' Andi admitted. 'It was ok to start with, but I don't think they ever really took to him; not like they have with you.' She wasn't really sure why she'd just said that. 'Probably my own fault for sharing so much of the things he does and says with them.'

'But why shouldn't you share things with your parents?' Andrew asked.

'Because it gives them the wrong opinion of him.' Even as she spoke, Andi couldn't believe what she was saying.

'Does it?' he asked raising an eyebrow. 'I think it says more about Drew than it does about them, and I like your parents.' He moved his hands away and reopened his laptop. 'They're very easy to talk to, like mine. I can tell them anything and they don't judge me, might tease me a bit now and again, sometimes get a telling off, but only if there's a good reason for it.'

'Drew's mum is a battle axe, and he doesn't really see his dad.' Andi hated her would be in laws.

'Carla is a spoilt princess I'm afraid.' Andrew rolled his eyes. 'I think they tell her she can do better than me. They're not impressed that I do gardening.'

'Do gardening?' she laughed. 'I thought you owned your own landscaping firm?'

'I do,' he replied proudly. 'I used to help my grandpa with his allotment and then we started doing a few odd jobs for people at weekends. I went to college and built up my own company from scratch.'

'That's bloody brilliant in my opinion,' Andi congratulated him. 'Why wouldn't your girlfriend and her family be proud of that?'

'They don't think I can keep her in the fashion she's become accustomed to.' Andi couldn't help but laugh at this, and she was relieved when Andrew joined in, breaking the previous tension that had been lurking overhead.

'It's the 2020s not the 1920s,' she said. 'What woman in this day and age relies on a man for that? In fact, what woman would want to? I earn my own money, have my own house, and pay my own way in everything. That's how I like it.'

'That's not Carla's view I'm afraid.' Andrew gave his full attention back to his laptop and Andi devoured the last piece of treacle tart thoughtfully.

'Why are you with her?' she asked, glancing at him as she placed her fork down on her plate quietly. She wasn't sure why she felt comfortable enough to ask him this but somehow, she did.

'I could ask the same question about you,' he replied simply, catching her eye above the laptop and holding her gaze. 'From what I know about Drew, I don't believe he deserves you.'

'I have the same feelings about Carla.' They stared at each other for what felt like an age, unspoken words exchanged between them, unspoken feelings conveyed in the moment as both of them addressed their own personal reasons for being with their respective partner and what struck Andi the most during this thought was that she couldn't really think of an answer as to why she was with Drew.

This thought whirled around her head for the rest of the day, while they uploaded the first video to the newly opened Pumpkin Patch Tik Tok account, while she drove home, hung some washing out and then as she sat with a cup of tea, watching a romance film on Netflix, she repeated the question aloud.

Why are you with him?

She couldn't answer the question, which terrified her a little. She loved him, of course she loved him, but did she? Did she really truly love him? Could she imagine being without him? She was quite shocked to admit to herself that if she was being totally truthful and honest with herself; she didn't think Drew's absence from her life would make much of a difference. In fact, a little voice suggested she might possibly be happier.

Wicked.

What a crazy thought. Of course she loved him, which is why she was so intent on keeping Andrew around in the hopes of making Drew jealous.

Are you sure you just don't like having Andrew around?

She was beginning to fall out with this little voice in her head and its random suggestions.

You know it's true. Why else do you get that sicky feeling in your stomach when you think about him and why do you keep having dreams about him naked?

'I do not have dreams about him naked,' Andi said out loud, causing Pumpkin to lift his head and cock it enquiringly to one side.

Do too.

'Do not.' She couldn't believe she was having an argument with the voice inside her own head. The trouble was it was telling the truth. Ever since that night when she'd called out his name in her sleep, her dreams had been filled with

Andrew, sometimes, perfectly normal but sometimes, oh sometimes, Fifty Shades of Grey was tame in contrast.

Andi put it down to her revived sex life with Drew and the frustration of not being completely fulfilled but the things that Andrew did to her in her dreams and in return the things she did to him made her wake-up sweating and often wet with desire. And she hoped against hope that she wouldn't call out his name again. She wasn't sure she'd be able to worm her way out of it again, especially now that Drew knew he was working with them.

'Why is some complete random working with you anyway?' Drew had asked. 'If you'd mentioned Tik Tok videos to me I'm sure I could have helped you, it is, after all, kind of what I do for a living.'

'It wasn't something we'd even thought about as a business,' Andi had explained. 'Mum suggested that she'd like to attract more customers from outside the area, but it was Andrew who suggested going on Tik Tok. He showed me the chip shop that went viral and just thought we could do something similar.'

'That was a fluke though,' he had scoffed. 'I could count on one hand the amount of businesses that have been successful on Tik Tok that quickly. It takes months, sometimes years, to build up a social media following.'

'Why can't you just be supportive for once?' Andi had complained.

'What on earth do you mean by that?' he had asked. 'I'm always supportive, I'm just being practical. You always get swept away by daydreams, living in your fantasy world of romance and roses, well life isn't like that.'

It had been a sobering moment for her, one that still echoed in her head and made her a little angry. 'What on earth was wrong with daydreams?' she had replied, and he had simply laughed and changed the subject.

Drew did that a lot, she was becoming to realise, squashing her dreams, her thoughts, anything happy in fact, anything that was maybe just hers or something in which he had an entirely different opinion on or perhaps thought was a bit silly, he would scoff at or ridicule in some way or another.

'Perhaps he's not the one for me after all,' she said to Pumpkin, ruffling his ears and as she said it a weight seemed to lift from her, a grey cloud that she didn't know was hanging over her disappeared, melting into the air like smoke. 'Now all I have to do is tell him.' And although this thought was one of dread and trepidation, it was also giving her a feeling of release and of renewal, excitement of new possibilities and not one of which was connected to Andrew in any way.

Oh who was she kidding. Andrew was the catalyst in all this, maybe not the driving force but definitely the spark that lit the fire, but it was Andi herself that was fanning the flames. Ever since Andrew had walked into her life that afternoon, sodden and carrying a wet Pumpkin in his arms, she had known he was the one for her, she just hadn't admitted it to herself before now. She was a huge believer in love at first sight, had been kidding herself that what she felt for Drew was love. How could you love someone that didn't share your views on anything? Had no interest in the things that interested you and was downright rude to you sometimes.

Yes, opposites attract but, in this instance, opposites repelled, like the same end of two magnets, coming together but at the last second, pushing each other away and no matter how hard you tried, you just couldn't make them stick.

'Well then, Pumpkin.' She sat up in her seat and the dog seemed to mimic her actions, lifting himself off the floor and sitting to attention. 'All it needs is for me to get my big girl pants on and tell Drew it's over.' This was easier said than done, especially as Drew came bounding into the house at that very moment with the largest bunch of flowers Andi had ever seen and the biggest grin on his face.

'I got it,' he shouted, thrusting the flowers into her hands, and then smacking a kiss on her astonished lips. 'They told us early.'

'Got what?' No sooner had she asked the question than she realised. 'The promotion?' He nodded.

'That's not all.' She couldn't remember a time when he'd been this happy. 'Sapphire and I get to head up our new branch.'

Andi prickled slightly at the name. 'Well that's brilliant.'

'Isn't it?' He took one of her hands in his. 'We can finally do it, Andi, we can finally buy that house together and settle down, just like you've always wanted to do. You'll find work easy enough and anyway; with my new salary you won't need to. You can be a housewife and mother when the kids come along.'

'You've lost me.' Although Andi wanted children, she didn't have the slightest inclination of giving up work. Lewis and Fran shared the responsibility for children equally and quite often brought Andi's nephew into the shop. He loved it and took great pleasure in stacking shelves with his grandad or helping his aunt in the field. 'Why do I need to look for another job?'

'It's a bit of a commute to York.'

Chapter 10

'York!' Andi couldn't believe what she was hearing. 'I can't move to York.'

'But you've always said how much you'd like to go there,' Drew recalled.

'For a holiday,' she said. 'But not to live. I live here, near my family, near my job.'

'You and your bloody job.' He threw his hands up in the air. 'You're a glorified shop assistant.' He took the flowers back out of her hands and chucked them on the floor. This startled Pumpkin who growled and went to stand next to Andi.

'How dare you?' she hissed. 'How dare you insult me and my family like that.'

'And now the precious family,' he scoffed. 'It isn't healthy to be in each other's pockets twenty-four seven.'

'Just because you have a crap relationship with your parents doesn't mean we all do.' Andi stroked Pumpkin's head to calm him. 'I love my mum and dad and I thoroughly enjoy spending as much time as I possibly can with them.'

'You're just scared to grow up and actually be a normal functioning adult,' he threw at her.

'I am not,' she retaliated.

'Prove it!' He picked the flowers back up and pressed them in her hands again, his anger subsiding as quickly as it came. 'Come with me to York.' She made to interrupt. 'Just to have a look around. See what you think, what jobs are available, property, that kind of thing.'

'But…'

'We could have a little mini break, just you and I.' He kissed her cheek then started nuzzling her neck. 'Book into a nice hotel, lovely bed just the two of us.' His hand slipped to caress her breasts. 'Walks around the city, meals out.'

Despite the earlier conviction to herself that she was going to break it off with him, she couldn't help but be won over by the thought of a few days away. The fact that during their entire relationship they hadn't stepped foot out of the Midlands was a big bone of contention between them, especially as COVID travel restrictions had been well and truly lifted but Drew was always too busy with work or worried he might be called in at a moment's notice.

'It's ok for you,' he would say whenever she suggested going away. 'Your mum and dad aren't going to sack you or look less favourably on you if you don't work overtime or go in if something high profile needs doing quickly.'

'Nobody HAS to do overtime, Drew.' Was always her reply. 'It's not the law and you can't be discriminated against because of it. I honestly don't know why you can't just do your hours like everyone else, come home at a reasonable time and take time off now and again.'

The situation had become much worse as he pursued promotion with him working long hours and most weekends but now maybe, just maybe, if he had succeeded in this goal, perhaps it would change him a little. Perhaps he would feel more secure and therefore relax. But if promotion meant moving to York, she wasn't sure this was something she could even contemplate.

It wasn't miles and miles away, but it was far enough that she couldn't just pop to her parents' house for a quick cup of tea or nip in and see her nephew on her way home from work. And also, she loved The Pumpkin Patch and not just because it was her parents' shop, although she knew that had a lot to do with it. But she liked where it was. Pickle Grove was a lovely place to live. Her favourite thing about the farm was the fields, the hours, and being able to take Pumpkin with her.

Don't forget Andrew.

There was that voice again.

'Sounds lovely,' she agreed, shaking her head internally to try and rid herself of the vision that had just popped in of Andrew smiling at her over the laptop.

'That's great.' He stopped kissing her. 'I'll leave you to sort out a hotel, something in the centre would be lovely, this weekend, if possible, next one at a push.' He pecked her on the cheek and made to go upstairs. 'I'm just going to grab a shower then we're meeting for drinks at The Shepherd.'

'Want me to join you?' she suggested, her insides all turned on after she'd been unable to rid her mind of the thought of

Andrew's hand caressing her thighs. She didn't even know where these random thoughts came from. He hadn't so much as touched her in an intimate way except maybe her hand but she had such erotic dreams about him she felt she knew every inch of his body already.

'No, it's just for work, you'll be bored.' Andi blushed as she realised. He thought she'd meant for drinks and not the shower, but she wasn't about to beg so just said OK and then spent the evening searching the internet for hotels in York, settling on one that had a view of the river. She paid a little extra for a room with a balcony, envisioning breakfast in bed, evening drinks and then texted her mum to ask if they could have Pumpkin for the weekend. The answer was of course yes and luckily her brother was free to cover her shifts.

Finally taking you away, is he? Her mum's text read, and Andi didn't mention anything about him moving away and just said it was to celebrate his promotion. **Maybe he'll realise what he's actually got now then.**

Drew was really late home and Andi was already in bed by the time he sauntered into the bedroom. He was clearly drunk and trying to be quiet, shushing himself when he made even the tiniest noise. She could hear him throwing off his clothes then felt him pull back the duvet and sidle in beside her, groping her breasts and shoving a hand between her thighs. She feigned sleep, sex with a drunk Drew was even less satisfying than with a sober Drew and he soon rolled over.

'You're no fun anymore,' he slurred, falling asleep almost instantly and snoring. Andi stepped out of bed and went down the stairs, silent tears rolling down her cheeks. Pumpkin padded over to her as she made herself a drink and she knelt down to kiss his forehead.

'What am I doing?' she asked him, and he looked at her with his green eyes and she knew then what she had to do. She marched up the stairs, switched on the bedroom light to the vehement annoyance of Drew who shouted and moaned and pulled the cover over his head. 'We need to break up.' There she'd said it. 'I want you out of my house and out of my life in the morning.'

'Ok,' came Drew's muffled response so she nodded to herself and went back down to the living room, sat on the sofa, relief easing her mind instantly.

She'd done it, she'd told him, she had expected a little more of a fight, but maybe he felt the same as her, maybe he'd just been pretending like she was, waiting for her to say something so he didn't have to. She put her head back on the sofa and sighed with such pleasure at the thought of Drew being out of her life that she got quite annoyed at herself for not having done it sooner.

All these months wasted on him and his narcissistic behaviour. Even earlier, with the hotel, he'd made out that he wanted a romantic break but really, he just wanted her to sort it all out and pay for it and yet again she'd fallen for it. Well not anymore. She'd bloody well go on that break all on her own. If it wasn't for the fact that the hotel didn't take pets, she'd have taken Pumpkin along, but she didn't want to be leaving him outside shops and he'd be much happier stopping with her parents and his beloved fields.

Feeling the lightest she had felt in a long time, she drained the last of her tea, left the cup on the side, because she could do that now without Drew shouting at her for being slovenly, called Pumpkin to heal and the pair of them went up to bed in the spare room. She heard Drew leave quite early the next morning, she was surprised he hadn't called her to at least say goodbye but judging by the slammed door he was obviously angry.

Reaching over to her phone she realised she was incredibly late for her shift in the shop. It must have been the relief and sleeping without a snoring boyfriend that had caused her to oversleep. She hurriedly fed Pumpkin, hastily cleaned her teeth, wondered why Drew had left his toothbrush but then it was only a toothbrush after all and then shot off in the car.

'I can't say I'm sorry,' Dennis said after she'd told them about Drew. 'He was absolutely no good for you.'

'He was worse than that Dennis,' Kathy proclaimed. 'He was an absolute waste of space, treated her like dirt, thought more about his work than our beautiful daughter. If I never see him again it will be too soon.'

'Blimey, Mum, don't hold back, will you?' Andi declared.

'And you make sure to get those locks changed so he can't get in and steal anything,' Kathy wagged her finger at Andi.

'He might be an arsehole Mum, but he wouldn't do that.' Andi couldn't help but laugh at her mum's comment.

'I wouldn't be so sure,' Kathy said. 'You and your dad get off back to the house, me and Kane will be ok for a few hours.'

'I think you're overreacting a bit, Mum,' Andi said.

'Do it for me, to put my mind at rest.' Kathy squeezed her hand reassuringly. 'Leave Pumpkin here, he's already asleep anyway.' This was of course true. Pumpkin was already curled up in his basket, his favourite toy dinosaur tucked under his chin.

'She won't rest, love, so may as well get it over and done with.' Dennis threw the van keys to her. 'Drop me off at the hardware store on High Street,' he said as she drove out of the farm gate. 'Then you get home and pop the kettle on.' He rubbed his hands together. 'And I hope you've got some biscuits in?' he asked hopefully. 'Your mum is on a diet again, so I don't get any treats either.'

This was always Kathy's way, she didn't need to lose weight but always, just a few months before Christmas she would decide that she was fat and needed to shed a few pounds and because she had absolutely no willpower, the only way she could do this was by not having anything naughty in the house so not only did her mum go on a diet but so did her dad.

'I think there's some chocolate digestives in the tin,' Andi told her dad as he stepped out of the van outside the shop.

'Plain chocolate?' Andi nodded and smiled as her dad's face lit up. 'That's my girl.' He shut the door and headed into the shop while Andi checked her blind spot and drove the half mile to her house.

'What on earth?' she asked herself as she pulled up outside her house, unable to get on the drive due to a rather flashy Mercedes being parked on it. She locked the van, walked up the path and turned the key in the lock. The house was in silence and looked exactly as she had left it. Perhaps someone was just being cheeky and using her drive she thought to herself then shrugged it off and headed into the kitchen. Switching on the kettle, she pulled out two mugs and the teapot her nan had bought her as a housewarming present. Her dad always liked his tea made in a pot.

'Who's car is that?' Dennis asked as he took his mug of freshly poured tea and headed into the living room. 'Bloody hell, Andi, did you get dressed in a hurry this morning?'

'What do you mean by that?' Andi followed her dad and her mouth fell open at the sight.

Chapter 11

Andi found herself confronted with a myriad of discarded clothes and shoes. She tentatively picked up a tiny black bra that looked about the right size for a pixie. 'This isn't mine,' she said, knowing full well that hers were the size of brick hods.

A female giggle followed by a male hushing sound from behind the sofa made her ears prick and she stormed over to the sofa, pulling it away from the wall to find the naked figures of Drew and Sapphire. She didn't know what she was most annoyed about, finding him with another woman or the fact that all these years he'd only ever had sex with her in a bed yet clearly, he was more adventurous with Sapphire.

'Get out of my house!' Andi shouted, pulling at Sapphire's legs, and dragging her along the floor. Sapphire screamed in panic and tried to cover herself with her hands.

'Drew, will you tell your girlfriend to get her hands off me,' she shrieked, grabbing the throw that lay across the back of the sofa and wrapping it around herself.

'I am NOT his girlfriend,' Andi replied, picking up the clothes and throwing them out of the now open front door. She was pleased to see her dad keeping his distance and allowing her to deal with it, but she knew he would wade in at any time if she needed him. 'We broke up last night.'

Drew's shoes followed the Louis Vuitton heels and a matching handbag.

'We did what?' Drew screwed his face up as he spoke, hitching himself along the floor with his hands over his bits. 'Is that what you were babbling on about?'

'Yes, Drew, that was what I was babbling on about,' she said, throwing his trousers at him. The buckle of his belt whacked him in the face, cutting his lip.

'That's assault that is,' Sapphire pointed. 'I'll call the police.'

'Oh I'll show you assault, love, if you don't get your scrawny little arse out of my house right now.' Andi stood in front of her and thankfully this was enough for Sapphire to step backwards out of the door, tripping over the throw as she went, and landing spread eagled on the lawn. A few of the neighbours must have heard the commotion and were now standing in their gardens pretending to have a sudden interest in horticulture.

'We can talk about this.' Drew stood in front of her as he hastily pulled his trousers on.

'Just get out, Drew.' She was determined not to cry and wanted him out of her sight before the inevitable tears started to fall.

'But Andi…' he protested.

'I think you should leave, Son.' Andi knew this was now the time for her dad to intervene. It wasn't that she wasn't strong enough to handle it on her own but being an emotional person, she knew it was going to end with her crying and she didn't want her tears of anger to be mistaken for weakness.

'But I love you,' Drew said as Dennis shoved the last of his things into his arms and almost frog marched him to the door.

'Well you've got a funny way of showing it.' Dennis shut the door in Drew's face as he was about to say something else, turned to Andi who immediately walked into her dad's arms and sobbed. 'I'm not going to say that he isn't worth your tears, he isn't but I'm not going to say it.'

'I'm not crying over him,' Andi said through sobs. 'I'm crying because I've been an idiot.'

'Hey now.' Dennis took her face in his hands gently and made her look at him. 'You are not and never have been an idiot. You loved him, you thought he loved you and that's all there is to it.'

'But…'

'No buts.' He pulled her against him and hugged her so tight that she couldn't breathe but it was the best feeling in the world and just what she needed at this precise moment in time. 'Let's get this lock changed, shall we?' Andi nodded through tears. 'And Dear God, your mum will be a nightmare to live with now, imagine that? She was right all along.'

Andi spent the rest of the day cleaning the house from top to bottom. Her dad went back to the shop after changing the lock on the front door and told her he'd walk Pumpkin and drop him back at the end of the day. She was grateful to have a few hours on her own to get her head straight.

She threw out all the bedding and considered torching it in the back garden along with all the bits he'd left but thought better of it. The thought that Drew may have shared them with another woman was too much for her and it was only the monetary expense of a new sofa that stopped her from throwing that out too, so she scrubbed it within an inch of its life and took out the new blanket she had been saving for Halloween and threw it over the cushions for good measure. The burnt orange colour gave her a hankering for autumnal walks with Pumpkin, crunchy leaves, and cosy jumpers.

Although she wasn't hungry in the slightest, she made herself eat cheese on toast for lunch and was grateful after for the comfort it gave her. There was something about grilled cheese that soothed the soul.

When her parents arrived just after six with Pumpkin and a takeaway curry, they found a very upbeat Andi and sat chatting around the dinner table sharing naan bread and poppadoms with the occasional crumb falling under the table and being gobbled up instantly by Pumpkin.

'Andrew was in the shop earlier.' Kathy managed to slide this into the conversation rather early on in the evening.

'That's nice.' Andi ignored the thrill that shot through her at his name. She was determined to just be friends with him. She'd been with Drew for so long that she'd forgotten what it was like to just be Andi and she was looking forward to finding it out. 'Is he ok?'

'He asked about you,' Kathy spoke with an insinuating tone and Andi knew exactly what her mum was implying.

'He has a girlfriend,' Andi stated, wiping a piece of naan around her plate to mop up the last of the sauce.

'You had a boyfriend up until this morning,' Kathy replied, receiving a harsh look from her daughter. 'All I'm saying is that things change.'

'He does seem like an awfully nice chap,' Dennis butted in.

'Not you as well,' Andi laughed, knowing that her parent's meddling was good natured. 'I don't need a man you know. I'm perfectly capable of being a fully functioning adult on my own.'

A statement that proved true for all of three hours when that evening the largest spider Andi had ever seen found its way into the living room, scaring her half to death and causing her to abandon the room completely, taking Pumpkin upstairs and sitting wrapped up in bed before falling asleep with the light on.

When she found that the spider had the audacity to still be there in the morning, she did the only thing possible in the circumstances and sucked it up into the hoover. Feeling very pleased with herself she ignored the fact that there was now a humungous spider trapped in her hoover bag and that at some point it would either escape or she'd have to empty the bag and she honestly didn't know which was worse.

She wasn't due into work till lunchtime, so she took Pumpkin for a walk around the town centre and bought some cakes from the bakery as a treat for everyone, she even popped an extra one in just in case Andrew turned up. Not that she was expecting him or even hoping to see him. Oh, who was she trying to kid. She longed to see him, to talk to him. She'd been resisting the urge to message him knowing full well how she'd feel if another girl had been messaging Drew and despite admitting to herself that she absolutely, one hundred percent fancied the pants off him, she was determined to keep any relationship with Andrew on a purely platonic footing.

It didn't stop her heart from skipping a little beat though when she saw his van parked in the shop car park as she arrived, and she almost ran up the driveway.

'Here she is now, early for a change.' Dennis looked at his watch as Andi walked in. Andrew turned to the door as she walked in and was she mistaken by how his face lit up at the sight of her?

'I was just showing your mum and dad a few sketches for our next production.' Even though the video had been up for a few days now, it had only received a few hundred views, one like and not even a comment. To say she was disappointed was an understatement and she knew Drew had been right, it would take more than one video to make them internet famous.

'We can't be borrowing the farm's combine harvester,' she laughed at the intricate drawings he had made of the sketch-by-sketch scene. 'And how on earth is Pumpkin going to drive it?'

Andrew joined in with her laughter. 'Yes, I might have got a bit carried away on that one.' He flicked through some more pages. 'I think Pumpkin is the secret weapon though.'

'Just have to think of another way of using him,' Andi said as Pumpkin, sensing something might be happening, almost ran off to his bed out the back.

'He doesn't seem overly enthusiastic,' Andrew remarked.

'Pumpkin's favourite things to do are eating and sleeping,' Dennis replied. 'Walks are permitted due to the fact that they usually involve treats during and after and he likes to chase squirrels but mostly eating and sleeping are the order of the day.'

'Andi broke up with Drew.' Kathy blurted this out to Andi's horror and placed a hand over her mouth as if she knew she shouldn't have said it but had been absolutely itching to.

'Mum!' Andi scolded, absolutely furious that her mum would say such a thing when it wasn't even vaguely related to the current topic of conversation.

'I'm sure Andrew doesn't wish to know about Andi's personal life.' Dennis tried to ease the tension that had suddenly occurred. 'Why don't you help me out the back with the potatoes?' He asked his wife, steering her by the shoulders when she went to protest.

'I'm sorry to hear that.' Andrew approached her after leaving his notebook on the counter and placing a comforting hand on her arm. 'Are you ok?'

'Truly?' he nodded at her question. 'Yes and no. It's a relief in a way but we were together for a long time, all through COVID but I just realised the other night that he didn't make me happy and after what I discovered yesterday, I clearly didn't make him happy either. I think it was just easier to stay together than making that decision to part.'

'May I ask what you discovered yesterday?' Andrew's voice was soft as he spoke, and she blurted out the whole sorry tale whilst crying on his shoulder.

'I don't even know why I'm crying,' she said, sniffing against his chest and catching the scent of woodsmoke as if he'd been near a bonfire recently. 'I broke up with him, I made the decision.'

'I think you're crying because of the relief maybe.' Andrew suggested. 'Or the frustration that he hadn't realised to start with and now he thinks it's just because you quite literally caught him with his pants down that you finished with him rather than just because you didn't want to be with him anymore.'

Andi giggled a little at his words. 'Pants down,' she repeated and giggled some more. 'Oh Andrew, it really was funny.' She broke into raucous laughter. 'Sapphire, wrapped in my favourite husky throw, lying spread eagled on the lawn.'

'I wish I'd been there to see it.' As she looked at him, she knew that he meant these words and not because he would have enjoyed seeing it but because he would have wanted to support her. 'I think I might have punched him though.' Andrew crooked his finger under her chin and lifted her head up and she stopped laughing instantly. 'He really didn't know what he had did he?'

Andrew looked at her with such sincerity in his gaze that she felt rooted to the spot. His brown eyes searched hers and she honestly didn't know what he hoped to find. A clue to her feelings? To his? She saw him glance at her lips, and she couldn't help but flick her tongue out slowly to wet them.

Without a word, Andrew shook his head, grabbed his notebook and was gone out the door.

'Has Andrew gone?' Kathy asked, walking in a few seconds later with mugs of tea.

'Yes, Mum, Andrew's gone.' And what made this statement so sad was that she didn't know if he'd ever be back again.

Chapter 12

'So you've had sex with Sapphire by default then.' Andi started choking on a grain of rice that went down the wrong way at Chloe's words.

'I've done what now?' Andi was coughing and spluttering so badly that one of the waiters came to check on her and handed her a glass of water which she sipped slowly while banging on her chest until the rice dislodged itself.

They were enjoying a quiet evening meal in the local pub, The Wheatsheaf, well, it was quiet until Chloe's little comment and Andi's coughing fit.

'You've had sex by default,' Chloe said again.

'I haven't the foggiest what you mean?' Andi tentatively placed another fork full of chilli and rice in her mouth and chewed it extra carefully.

'You haven't heard of sex by default?' Andi shook her head. 'You had sex with Drew, and he had sex with Sapphire, so you've had sex with her by default.'

'You aren't making any sense.' Andi's head was hurting from trying to work this little nugget of information out.

'Do I have to spell it out?' Chloe hissed under her breath.

'I think you do yes.' Andi was quite certain that Chloe was going to have to spell it out because she really couldn't fathom how having sex with someone by default was even a thing.

'So you've had sex with Drew.' Chloe had lowered her voice, so Andi was having to lean closer over the table to hear her.

'Yes,' Andi whispered.

'And Drew has had sex with Sapphire.' Chloe was speaking even quieter now.

'Obviously,' Andi said rather indignantly.

'So, his willy has been in…'

'CHLOE!' Andi couldn't believe what her friend had just said and her voice was far louder than she had anticipated, a few people in the room turned to look at her and she smiled apologetically at them while Chloe laughed into her drink. 'That's disgusting.'

'True though.' Chloe raised her glass to Andi who was by now, so disgusted at this thought implanted in her mind that she was going through all her ex-boyfriends and trying to remember their exes.

'Are you sure it's a real thing or just something that lives in Chloe's world?' Chloe was renowned for coming up with weird and wacky things.

'Well, if it's not a real thing it should be.' Chloe poured more wine into her glass and went to top up Andi's.

'Best not,' she said, placing a hand over the rim. 'Early start in the morning.'

'Oh yes, your solo trip to York.' Chloe poured the rest of the bottle into her glass. Pumpkin had already been left with Kathy and Dennis so Andi could just get up and go in the morning. 'If I wasn't working, I'd be coming with you.'

'I'm actually looking forward to some time on my own if I'm honest.' This was no insult to Chloe; she loved her company, but this was something she wanted to do on her own.

'I totally get it,' Chloe waved her hand in front of her. 'I love Miley, I really do but she's constantly there and sometimes I just want to walk round the house naked without being jumped on every five minutes or go to sleep having a cuddle instead of having her tongue on my bits every night.'

'Every night?' Andi raised her eyebrows.

Chloe nodded. 'And sometimes she wakes me up in the night to do it as well.'

'And that's a bad thing?' Andi asked. 'Drew never did that to me. No, actually, I tell a lie, he did once, when he got pissed at his brother's wedding and we stayed at a hotel for the night.'

'That's totally out of order but honestly my love, you can have too much of a good thing.' Chloe placed her knife and fork down neatly on the plate.

'Things ok with the two of you?' Andi sensed a little tension.

'Oh yeah, she's just very sexual,' Chloe stated and Andi felt a tinge of jealousy. Here was her, just come out of a relationship with very little sex and Chloe was getting too much.

'Perhaps you should have a word with her?' she suggested much to Chloe's chagrin.

'Dear Lord, she'd be mortified,' Chloe declared. 'She thinks I like it.'

'And do you like it?' Andi asked. 'Really, honestly like it?'

'Yes,' Chloe admitted. 'But not ALL the time.'

'Then tell her,' Andi remarked. 'If I've learnt one thing from the past few weeks it's to be truthful with yourself and others. Only one person can make you happy and that's you. Pretending to be something or someone you are not, isn't healthy for any relationship, romantic or otherwise.'

'Very philosophical I must say.' Chloe eyed her over the glass. 'And how is Andrew these days?'

'This has nothing to do with Andrew.' Andi wished now that she had taken up the offer of more wine as her glass was empty.

'Pull the other one it's got a pumpkin on it,' Chloe snorted. 'This has everything to do with Andrew. If it wasn't for him dashing into your life like some knight in shining armour, you'd be blissfully unaware of how unhappy you actually were with Drew, even though everyone else could see it and you'd certainly be none the wiser about his affair.' Andi's face fell. 'I'm sorry to upset you and remind you about Drew, but the fact of the matter is, he was cheating on you.'

'Thank you, Chloe, I'm very much aware of that fact.' Andi really was wishing she had more wine in her glass now.

'Don't you be getting upset about it now,' Chloe warned. 'He's not worth the shit on your shoe.'

'The what on my what?' Andi looked at her friend once again. 'Is this another Chloeism?'

'Stop changing the subject.' Chloe wagged a finger at her. 'He was an absolute piece of shit before the affair and is an even bigger piece of shit now.'

'I am fully aware of how big a piece of shit Drew is,' Andi remarked. 'What I'm upset about is how bloody long I wasted in finding out.'

'But that doesn't matter now,' Chloe soothed. 'What matters now is you.' She placed a hand on Andi's and squeezed it tightly. 'And also how we get rid of Andrew's girlfriend.' She laughed at this, and Andi joined in. 'No, honestly, it's all about you now, Hun.'

'Well I'll drink to that.' Andi picked up her glass and then realising it was empty, laughed but still clinked it against Chloe's. 'Cheers.'

When her alarm went off at six the next morning, Andi was grateful she hadn't drunk anymore alcohol that night because her head was already feeling fuzzy, and she had the worrying thought that she might be coming down with a cold.

'Bloody typical,' she muttered to herself before jumping in the shower quickly, rubbing herself dry and chucking on her comfy joggers and a jumper. She quickly threw a few bits and bobs into a bag; she was only going for one night but packed five pairs of pants just in case.

It looked like a straightforward drive up the A1 to York, she decided against the motorway option, and by seven was in the car and on her way. She opted to listen to the radio rather than the playlist on her phone and stopped at some services about halfway there. She could have carried on driving; she'd only been going for an hour, but she'd already decided that she would have breakfast on route and treated herself to a full English and her first Pumpkin Spiced Latte of the season.

Feeling refreshed and incredibly excited, the last fifty miles flew by and even the fact that it was hammering down with rain by the time she reached York, did nothing to diminish her spirits. She parked in the park and ride car park on the outskirts of town, grabbed her handbag and umbrella and headed on the bus into the town centre.

Despite the weather, the town was already bustling, and Andi's first stop was to York Minster. This was obviously everyone else's first stop too because it was incredibly busy, but she paid her entrance fee and then stood in awe at her surroundings.

Andi had always loved cathedrals, from her very first visit to the ruins of Coventry when she was six and had visited with school when they were learning about World War Two and then her most recent visit to Gloucester just before COVID when her and Chloe had walked round in black cloaks pretending they were at Hogwarts.

There was just something utterly majestic about cathedrals. All the history that they had seen, all the people over the years that had visited or worshipped. Here she was, a tiny blip in a timeline. Hundreds of years before her and hundreds of years ahead of her. It certainly made you feel humble, looking at the vaulted ceiling and pillars.

Due to the heavy rain, the tower was closed but Andi still spent almost three hours wandering around and taking in the atmosphere. It amazed her how quiet it remained in there despite the echoing chambers and all the people whispering. She'd sat in one of the pews for a while, just pondering life and love and after seeing a notice for a local pumpkin picking farm, this had given her an idea for The Pumpkin Patch, and she sent a quick text to her parents about it in case she forgot later on.

Kathy sent her a photo of Pumpkin out on his walk and informed her that he'd had sausage, bacon, and egg for breakfast, had slept on their bed last night and was currently looking for a squirrel that had decided to jump in front of him.

This made her smile, and she was glad to see that the rain had eased a little when she headed back outside, so took advantage and walked by the river. Even though it was only a few hours since breakfast, she was ravenous and stopped off for tea and cake, watching the world go by.

The little break away was definitely what she needed. Time to think, time to just be Andi. She found her hotel and they informed her that her room was ready, so she collected the key and then got the bus back to her car and drove to the hotel. Why she hadn't done this in the first place she didn't know but at least now she was all parked up and ready.

Her room was beautiful, it overlooked the river just as described and the double bed, although small looked incredibly comfortable and she couldn't resist throwing herself on to it and snuggling in the duvet. She threw open the doors and stepped onto the balcony, breathing in the damp air made her cough a little and she thanked earlier Andi for having the forethought to pack her fleece lined jacket. She wasn't a fan of coats, she found them a bit cumbersome, but this was the cosiest thing she owned, and she loved it when the weather turned, and she could wear it once again.

She quickly unpacked her meagre belongings and wished she was staying for longer but promised herself that from now on, she would do things for her and start putting herself first more.

It was raining again when she left the hotel and as she was heading to the shops, decided that hood up would be best compared to fighting through crowds with an umbrella. With a rucksack on her back she soon found herself in The Shambles.

Andi looked around in awe, the old timber clad buildings looked like they shouldn't even be able to stand up, they leaned towards each other and seemed to be staying up because they wanted to rather than because they should. The street was cobbled, and she felt as if she'd just stepped back to Tudor times.

The rain was beating down really fast now, and she found herself outside a curious looking shop that seemed to only be selling ornamental ghosts. There was all sorts of colours, two basic sizes that she could see but upon peering in through the window she could see so many different designs scattered around the shop. She looked up and saw the sign, The York Ghost Merchants. There were a few people inside, so she headed to the door.

'Excuse me.' A rather annoyed voice came from behind her, and she felt a tap on her shoulder. 'You'll find that there's a queue.' She turned to see a lot of very bedraggled looking people standing in line that seemed to stretch all the way down the lane.

'I'm so sorry. I didn't realise.' She pushed her hood back a little so she could apologise to the man who had spoken to her. 'Andrew? What on earth are you doing here?'

Chapter 13

'Next please.' There was now a lady at the door to the shop. She wore an overly long grey apron and smart, almost Victorian in style jacket.

Andrew ushered the couple behind him to go ahead.

'Don't be silly,' Andi insisted. 'You go on in. I'll join the back. You must have been waiting for ages.'

'About two hours.' Andi could see he was hesitant to leave her but the desire to complete the errand he was obviously on was too much and he headed inside. Andi had no such urgency to stand in the queue, in the rain for two hours so loitered around for a few minutes until Andrew reemerged. 'Drink?' he suggested, and she nodded.

They headed into a lovely café and fell lucky just as someone was leaving and grabbed a table by the window that had a wonderful view of the cobbled street outside. Andi shrugged herself out of her jacket, being extra careful not to shower the man sitting behind her with rain and placed it gingerly on the back of her chair. Although Andrew was wearing a zip up coat, he reached his hands up and pulled it over his head, giving Andi an unexpected glimpse of a nicely toned chest and a small smattering of dark hair.

She shook her head to clear the vision of herself resting on said chest, running her hand over his skin and down to his belly button. Unbuttoning his jeans and…

'What can I get you both?' Andi hadn't noticed the young man standing next to the table with a notebook and pen, poised to take their order.

'Tea for me please and a slice of parkin.' Andi looked at Andrew as if he were speaking a different language. The slight accent he had before suddenly become thick and glorious, emphasising his vowel sounds.

'That sounds lovely.' Even though she'd already had cake earlier, another slice sounded perfect, and parkin was always welcoming with its warm, gingery tones.

'What are you doing in York?' Andrew asked, his normal accent returning the instant the lad had left.

'I could ask you the same thing,' Andi replied.

'Birthday present for my mum,' he held up the small bag. 'She collects these, and I get her one every year now since they opened.' He handed her the bag. 'I kept missing their online releases so had to make an emergency trip up here. Have a look if you like. They're really smashing.'

Andi looked inside the bag and took out the intricately designed box. It looked like it had a map printed on the outside and this was mirrored on the tissue paper that wrapped the ghost inside. She unwrapped it carefully and was surprised at how lovely and smooth it felt to her touch. Tiny little holes had been made for eyes and it was a very basic ghost shape, the kind you would have drawn as a child but somehow that only added to it. A more complicated design would have detracted from it. This particular one reminded her of a stormy sky.

'It's beautiful. There was a lovely orangey one in the window, reminded me of Pumpkin.' She wrapped it up again carefully. 'Do people really wait that long to go in the shop though?'

'Oh yeah.' Andrew put the bag back on the floor. 'The shop is so small that only a few people can get in at a time, but I think they're opening new premises soon. Mum has been after one of those stormy ones for ages.'

'So you've come all the way here just for that?' Andi was impressed.

'Nothing is too much trouble for my mum.' Andrew moved the sugar bowl away from the middle of the table to allow the waiter room to place the newly arrived tea pot and cups and Andi's eyes widened at the slab of parkin that was now sitting in front of her. 'Yorkshire servings,' he said, laughing at her expression.

'I mean, I like cake but…' She really did like cake but after a huge fry up and a rather large muffin not long ago she was feeling rather full. 'It is delicious though.' Despite the full feeling, Andi devoured it.

'Give me a girl than can eat a good slice of cake any day.' Andi didn't know why, but she felt this may have been a dig at Carla. 'You haven't told me why you're in York.'

Andi found herself telling him the whole sorry tale. There was something about Andrew that made her want to share with him, maybe even overshare as she found herself telling him everything, how Drew used to make her feel fat and awkward, his lack of sex drive, and through it all, Andrew just sat there, taking it all in.

'And there you have it.' She felt so light, not even Chloe had been told some of the things she'd just said to Andrew.

'If you were my girlfriend, I wouldn't let you out of the bedroom.' Andi looked at him over the table thinking that he was making a joke but the way that he was looking at her over the cups was definitely not funny. 'You deserve to be loved and cherished, treated with respect and Dear God, he must have been blind not to see how sexy you are.'

Andrew's face had taken on a look somewhere between immense desire and absolute anger. His eyes matched the storminess of the ghost he'd just purchased for his mum and Andi felt the irresistible urge to kiss it away. She tried to swallow but her mouth was so dry that it was impossible. How did she reply to that? Why was he even saying such things to her? Here? In the middle of a café.

'Can I get you a refill?' The waiter asked, hovering next to the table with a pot of hot water.

'I think we're ok, thank you,' Andrew said and then as soon as the waiter had gone, he grabbed his coat and bag. 'I'm sorry, I can't do this.' And he was gone out of the café, off down the street into the rain without even bothering to put his jacket on.

The day had lost its charm for Andi after that. She sat in the café till it closed and then headed back to her hotel where she sat on the balcony, staring out at the rain and drinking the entire contents of the mini bar. How dare he make her feel like that? She'd vowed never to let a man make her feel this way again and certainly not so quickly after Drew but here she was, yet again, drowning her sorrows over a man.

Then maybe you should tell him. The voice in her head that was clearly fuelled by red wine suggested.

Well then maybe I will. The little voice answered and before she knew it, she had picked up her phone and texted Andrew.

In her mind the message was clear and concise but when she read it back the next day with an aching head and thankfully an error message saying it hadn't been sent, she realised she'd basically sent him a booty call.

The smell of breakfast wafting up the stairs made her heave, and she spent a few minutes with her head over the toilet and then after a shower felt decidedly better. York had lost its appeal and she decided to make her way home after forcing a slice of dry toast down her neck and baulking at the mini bar bill.

The radio did little to lift her spirits and after a quick toilet break on the services, she plugged her phone in but Celine Dion's All by Myself came on and she turned the stereo off rather angrily and drove in silence the whole way home.

She didn't tell anyone she was back. Let them all think she was having the jolly time that she should have been having.

She couldn't bear the sympathetic looks and sighs from everyone. No, just pretending was the way to go.

After popping some popcorn in the microwave and snuggling under her blanket on the sofa, she searched Netflix and found herself watching three wonderfully cheesy romance films and shouting at the screen when the male lead realised that actually he does love her, and they lived happily ever after.

'But where's my happily ever after?' she asked the empty room and sobbed into the bowl of unpopped kernels.

Andi must have fallen asleep because it was dark when she woke up and she had absolutely no idea what time it was or even how long she'd been asleep for. The TV had switched itself off, her phone was wedged under her bum and there were bits of stray popcorn stuck to her cheeks.

Car headlights flooded into the pitch-black living room, and she looked out of the window. They were so bright that they blinded her, and she couldn't work out who's car it was. Maybe it was her dad with Pumpkin she thought and almost ran to the door, flinging it open.

'I've missed you so much.' Andi knelt with her arms open, but instead of a huge red husky running into them she was met with a pair of legs.

'Well that's a lovely welcome.' She looked up at the male voice. Of all the people she thought would be standing there, Andrew was most definitely the least likely.

'What are you doing here?' she asked, ignoring the hand he offered to help her up with and instantly regretting it as she almost stumbled into him as she stood. 'How do you know where I live?'

'Can I come in?' he asked. The rain from yesterday was still beating down and she stepped inside the house, leaving the door open for him to follow. He wiped his shoes on the mat and then took them off before running his hand through his now slightly damp hair. 'I've come to apologise.'

'For what?' she asked. She'd done a lot of thinking on her drive home in the silence. It wasn't Andrew's fault that she fell for him. He hadn't asked her to, he had a girlfriend, she'd known that practically from the start. She should be happy that he was such an honourable man that he wouldn't cheat unlike Drew.

'For running out on you like that.' He was looking at the floor and shuffling his feet from side to side. 'It was very rude.'

'You don't owe me an explanation, or an apology.' Andi remarked, trying to sound flippant. She was going to have to harden her heart against this man because he was making it so hard not to fall in love with him.

'But I do.' He took hold of her hand as she made to turn away and as he did a warm sensation shot up her arm and into her heart. Oh Dear God, she was already in love with him.

'I can't do this Andrew.' She turned to look at him, tears suddenly welling in her eyes at the realisation of her feelings for him. She hadn't meant to fall in love with him, hadn't expected to so soon and so hard but she knew she had, and it made her heart feel like lead to know that she couldn't have him.

He was still holding her hand. 'I can't be without you, Andi.'

'You have to be, I won't be anyone's bit on the side,' she whispered, looking up at him through tear-splashed eyes. His face was full of longing, but she knew what she had to do. She reached up and placed a tender kiss upon his lips, pulling away quickly before they both did something they would regret. 'Close the door when you leave,' she said and walked slowly and sadly up the stairs.

Part of her hoped he would follow but she knew that he wouldn't, he was too much of a gentleman for that. She heard the door close after a few moments and his car drive away. When she came downstairs a little later there was a box on the table in the hallway and when she opened it, she found the orange ghost she had seen in the shop window.

Chapter 14

'But why did he come round? How did he know where you lived?' Chloe asked as they sat in her living room the next day. Miley was at work and Pumpkin was in the garden playing with Chloe's dog Pepper.

'Does this answer your question?' Andi showed Chloe the message that had miraculously sent itself to Andrew.

'Good job you didn't send it to Drew,' Chloe laughed. 'Only you could do something as daft as that. He must have thought you had the funnies with him from your tone but then you're practically begging him for sex.'

'Don't!' Andi was still mortified. 'And I think my mum told him where I lived, accidentally she says but who knows with my mum,' Andi rolled her eyes.

'Leaving that ghost for you though,' Chloe hugged herself. 'It's quite romantic really when you think about it and its obvious, he has feelings for you.'

'It doesn't matter that he has feelings for me though,' Andi said. 'He won't act on them, and I don't want him to.' Chloe gave her a look. 'Well, obviously I want him to act on them, but I don't want to do to Carla what Drew and Sapphire did to me.'

A key turning in the lock made them both look to the door and Miley walked in looking tired. Pepper and Pumpkin bounded in at the sound and almost knocked her flying as they jumped on her and started licking her.

'Oh hi, Andi,' Miley said cheerfully. 'I didn't know you were coming round.'

'You're back early,' Chloe stated, dragging the two dogs away who immediately ran back outside.

'Teds had a right hissy fit and sent us all home.' She threw herself on the sofa. 'The software bug that was meant to have been fixed over the weekend is still glitching so no one can get anything to work properly so we've just been twiddling our thumbs waiting for the IT department to pull their finger out and in the end, Ted just shouted at us to go home. We didn't need telling twice I can tell you.'

'I'll pop the kettle on and make us all a nice cuppa.' Chloe stood up.

'Don't worry about me.' Andi went off to the garden and called Pumpkin in. 'We'd best be getting home anyway,' she clipped on his lead.

'You don't need to go on my account,' Miley said. 'I'm just going to have a nice bath and chill in front of the TV.'

'Honestly it's fine,' Andi replied. 'I've got so much stuff to sort out what with me and Drew breaking up.' She had absolutely nothing to sort out and Chloe knew it but luckily Miley didn't and so she just nodded. Although she liked Miley, she always felt like she was intruding in the relationship when she was around and found it much easier to just spend time with Chloe when she was on her own. Yes, this meant far less opportunities since both of them had been in a relationship, but it did mean the time they spent together was far more meaningful.

'No more butt texting,' Chloe reminded her as she walked Andi to the door.

'I promise.' She kissed her friend goodbye on the cheek and then headed home. 'What am I going to do with my time now?' she asked Pumpkin who looked up at her as they walked. Then she remembered the idea she'd had in York and started to work through it in her head. Oh she wished she could talk about it with Andrew, he'd know exactly how to sort it, but she couldn't and that was that.

'Pumpkins by post?' Dennis looked at her over his mug of tea. It was Tuesday and she was filling her parents in on her idea. 'How on earth is that going to work?'

'Not just by post but in person too,' Andi replied. 'We let the public come and pick their own pumpkins. It's all the rage these days, I've seen lots of places advertising it and then they'll have to come in the shop to pay.'

'I'm not having people trudging all over my nice fields.' Dennis didn't sound enthralled by the idea. 'Plus, we haven't got enough staff to be walking round willy nilly and cutting pumpkins every five minutes.'

'You're not listening, Dad,' Andi insisted. 'We harvest the pumpkins as usual but instead of just putting them in the shop or selling them on we put them in the barn. We can still leave a few in the fields though.'

'I don't see the difference.' Dennis took a slurp of his tea and shook his head.

'Because we make it different.' Andi showed him a few photos on her phone. 'In an ideal world we'd let them wander around the fields but that's not possible, so we get hay bales and make scarecrows and decorate the barn, so it feels like an experience and not just rocking up to the shop and buying a pumpkin.'

'We could do a scarecrow competition?' Kathy suggested to which Andi readily agreed. 'Even pumpkin carving.' Andi could tell her mum was fully on board.

'Wheelbarrows instead of shopping baskets,' Preeti offered.

'What do you think Dad?' Andi asked and squealed when her dad nodded.

'But what's these pumpkins by post?' Dennis asked again. 'Some of them this year are bloody huge.'

'Now, that's where our very own pumpkin comes into play.' Andi pulled out a piece of paper that she'd hastily sketched on the night before. 'We can use Tik Tok for this, I've seen people packing sweet orders and crystal orders live so I thought we could go one step further and use Pumpkin.'

'You've lost me,' Kathy admitted. 'Are you suggesting we use Pumpkin to pick people's pumpkins?' Andi nodded. 'How? Why?'

'It's just a gimmick really.' She showed them the sketch of Pumpkin in a pumpkin hat sniffing out pumpkins in the field whilst being filmed. 'Andrew said people love dogs.' Her breath caught for a second at his name, but she hid it well and carried on. 'I've done a bit of research and I reckon we can package and post for around five pounds, or people can collect. Add five pounds on for our time and then the actual pumpkin so maybe fifteen ninety-nine.'

Dennis spat his tea into his cup. 'No one is going to pay that much for a pumpkin when they go to the supermarket and pick one up for two quid.'

'Ah, but Dad, you're not getting it.' Dennis, Kathy, and Preeti looked at Andi. 'This will be a pumpkin, picked by Pumpkin and delivered from The Pumpkin Patch.'

'You're making me want one,' Preeti laughed.

'But how will a dog pick a pumpkin?' Kathy repeated. 'It's not like it's meat.'

'Watch and learn mother dearest.' Andi took three marrows off the shelf and placed them on the floor, she then took a treat out of her pocket and placed it under one of them. 'Pumpkin, here boy.' Pumpkin ran into the room. 'Find the biscuit,' she asked him and immediately the dog sprang into action, his nose in full sniffing mode until he found the treat. But because it was under the marrow, he had to push it with his nose. 'With a pumpkin and in the field, it will look like he's chosen it himself but in reality, we already have.'

'So that will mean you can keep the size of the pumpkin to a small one,' Dennis confirmed.

'We can film a few live each day, weather permitting,' Andi suggested, maybe pre-record some as well depending on how popular it is.'

'I think it sounds really intriguing,' Kathy admitted. 'I wasn't sure what you were bleating on about when you texted from York but now, I can see it so much clearer.' She paused for a second. 'How was York by the way, you've been ever so quiet since you got back, and you didn't send any photos except for The Minster.'

'I completely forgot to take any.' This wasn't technically a lie Andi thought. 'I was just so busy it slipped my mind.' She was feeling so good about things at the minute that she really didn't want to have to explain about Andrew and York. She knew her mum especially would spin it round somehow and try and make it into something positive.

And truth be told she was already missing him. She knew that sounded daft, after all, he'd only been in her life for a few weeks and it hadn't even been two days since she'd seen him but the finality of how they left it, well, how she left it made her want to sob whenever she thought about it so she decided the best thing to do was not think about it and distract herself with work.

She'd already talked to the farmer about borrowing some hay bales and had spent hours on the internet sourcing decorations and boxes. She'd even found a company to produce some personalised stickers, far cheaper than personalised boxes but still giving the personal touch.

Andi hoped she was right in all this, after all, their little Tik Tok video had, let's face it, been a total disaster but then honestly what had they expected to happen? The group would see it and come visit the shop? She laughed at this but knew deep down that's exactly what she had hoped would happen. As if they'd fly all the way over to Britain just for that.

No, this was definitely a much better idea and far more practical. Also, she'd already thought of other ideas if it took off. Pumpkin picking Christmas Trees, the farm always sold them every year so she'd have to split profits with them but that wouldn't matter. Pumpkin dressed as Cupid for Valentine's Day, the Easter Bunny, in fact, she'd got something in mind for every season, she just wished she could have shared it with Andrew, he'd have loved it.

The thought of Andrew made her sad again, so she grabbed Pumpkin's lead and went for a stroll through the fields, her dad joining her.

'What's up then?' he asked as soon as they were out of earshot of the shop. 'I know it's not Drew.'

'I'm fine, Dad, honestly,' she turned to him with a smile plastered on her face.

'You are far from fine my lovely.' He took her empty hand in his. 'And you need gloves on, your fingers feel like ice.'

'I need to look them out, the cold weather has kind of come on us quickly hasn't it.' She pretended to be interested in something Pumpkin had found but her dad wasn't fooled.

'It's Andrew, isn't it.' Dennis didn't even phrase this as a question.

Andi shook her head. 'I'm just being silly, Dad. He's got a girlfriend and that's that.'

'Up until a few days ago, you had a boyfriend,' he declared. 'Things change.'

'But I shouldn't be wishing myself into another relationship so soon and I shouldn't be hoping that someone else's relationship is going to fail.' She kicked a stone on the ground.

'I always find that things have a habit of working themselves out when I'm not trying to help them along.' Andi looked at her dad's face. 'Just enjoy what you have now, and you'll find, somewhere down the line, everything will fall into place, without you even knowing about it.'

'Like you and Mum?' Dennis nodded.

'I think your mum had a bit more say in us getting together than I'm fully aware of, even to this day but I don't just mean in relationships,' he continued. 'Life carries on, whether we want it to or not, what we have to do is appreciate it. Even the bad things help us to grow and appreciate the good things.'

They walked for a while, Dennis declaring that some of the pumpkins were ready for picking and announcing this to the shop upon their return.

'Oh good.' Kathy rubbed her hands together with glee. 'I'll text Andrew and tell him, he was desperate to come and help with the harvest.' And before Andi could tell her no, she'd disappeared into the back room with her phone in hand.

Chapter 15

'I can't believe you just did that, Mum,' Andi scolded when she reappeared in the front of the shop. 'You can't keep doing this. It's not fair on him or me come to mention it.'

'But you like each other,' Kathy insisted. 'It's so obvious to everyone.'

'When are you going to listen to me?' Andi softened her voice. 'I do like him, yes.' She admitted and it felt good to say it out loud. 'And I'm pretty certain he likes me.'

'There you go then,' Kathy beamed.

'But!' Andi put her hand up. 'And this is a big but Mum. Andrew has a girlfriend and has made it perfectly clear to me that this is something that won't be changing anytime soon. He loves Carla and is far too much of a decent bloke to cheat on her and I wouldn't want him to.'

'You loved Drew,' Kathy said simply.

'Once upon a time long ago I did,' Andi replied. 'But his cruelness killed any love I had for him; I'd just failed to see it and was hanging on to a memory, an ideal maybe.'

'Well I think that's a very honest and grown-up admission.' Dennis put a fatherly arm around her shoulders and hugged her tight.

'I'm sorry, Andi,' Kathy stepped towards her daughter and threw her arms around her. 'I'll stop my meddling.'

Andi laughed. 'I very much doubt it, Mum, but the sentiment is appreciated.'

'Afternoon family.' Lewis appeared at the door. 'Bloody hell, what have I missed? Someone died?'

'No, no,' Kathy fussed. 'Everyone's fine, just having a moment.'

'Thank goodness for that.' He was carrying what appeared to be cardboard. 'I've picked up a few different boxes to see which one's will work best. Now, thinking on your idea, Andi, I thought that even if they come and collect themselves it might be nice to pop it in a box anyway.' He placed the flat boxes on the counter and started building as he talked. 'We could use the slightly flimsier ones for collection, not handles as we want people holding them properly and not having their pumpkin dropping out and smashing on the floor. And these sturdy ones will be perfect for posting. They're already double lined walls and wrapped in bubble wrap I think they'll suffice.'

'It looks like Pumpkins by Post is a goer then,' Dennis shouted.

'And The Pumpkin Picking Patch,' Andi added, and they all clinked their mugs together except for Lewis who was most put out that he didn't have one.

Despite Andi insisting that her mum text Andrew back, she refused saying that it would appear rude and if he showed up then she'd just have to grin and bear it this time but promised not to meddle anymore and just let him be.

'If he wants to come, Mum, it's up to him.' Andi had said to which Kathy had nodded. Andi had resigned herself to the fact that she probably would never see him again. After all, they'd lived in the same place all these years and she'd never bumped into him before. Life was funny like that. Always seeming to send you the right person at the right time, or maybe the wrong time in this case. But no, she scolded, Andrew had been what she needed to give her the courage and belief in herself to end her relationship with Drew and she would look back on their brief time together with fondness. Now, if she could just stop having the erotic dreams about him that would help.

She had decided to throw herself into the tasks ahead with every ounce of gusto she could manage. She spoke to the farmer about the barn, and he was so enthusiastic about her ideas that she was able to get started straight away and he offered to pay for some signs to go outside and in the town centre and promised to spread the word as much as he could.

By Friday, the barn was almost ready. Straw had been lain on the floor to give a rustic feel and also help with muddy boots should the weather turn wet. Hay bales were stacked around along with borrowed racking to allow for pumpkins to be placed here, there, and everywhere so children and adults alike could go hunting for their perfect specimen.

They had decided to pre-price the pumpkins beforehand, so people knew exactly how much they were spending. There was nothing worse than getting to the till and someone being embarrassed by how much they'd spent. Andi had spent hours weighing and writing out little brown tags before tying them to the pumpkins and then used little Halloween stencils to cut out shapes on the tag.

She really couldn't believe why they'd never thought of doing something like this before now. It seemed such a simple idea but when she thought about it, it was maybe only the past few years that pumpkin picking had started to become popular in the UK. Families wanted something different, something they could enjoy together, whatever the age.

Andi was going to bed achingly but happily tired each night through sheer exhaustion. She was at the farm from early hours to late at night and she gratefully slumped under the duvet, Pumpkin curled up beside her, asleep as soon as her head hit the pillow.

The problem with this was the dreams. In her exhausted state her mind wandered freely and completely out of control. Andrew featured heavily in all of them and in various stages of undress. Sometimes she could attribute the dreams to things she had done that day, or something she had seen on the TV, but others were just pure lust and desire.

'Do you need a hand putting them out?' Kane asked as he delivered a fresh load of pumpkins to Andi who was just starting to place the now labelled ones around the barn.

'No, I should be ok thanks.' She wanted to do this bit herself. She'd planned in her head exactly how she wanted it to look, where and how she would hide the pumpkins, how she was going to hang the decorations and was so excited to start taking the photos and advertising and maybe even getting their first customers, after all, it was only a week till October now. Thankfully, if kept cool, pumpkins had a really long shelf life, it was only once they were carved that the clock started ticking on them.

She started by placing the larger pumpkins lower down, spreading them around the barn, making sure that they were placed out of the way of feet, they didn't want people trampling or kicking the stock. There was a few extra-large ones and she decided that these would look best in a group with some smaller ones balancing on them.

Andi had already decided to have a couple of carved ones at the entrance, these she had chosen from ones that weren't quite so perfect or maybe had dents in them already and she had already placed a small pile by the table next to where the temporary till would be. Picking up the knife, she started slicing around the top where she had drawn a line around the top.

'This looks amazing,' a familiar voice from the doorway spoke and as she looked up, she lost all concentration and caught her finger with the knife.

'Ouch.' Andi immediately put her finger in her mouth.

'Oh God, I'm so sorry. Are you ok?' Andrew was by her side in a heartbeat and took hold of her hand, lifting it to lips, kissing it profusely. 'I didn't mean to startle you.' He was looking at her fingers, examining each one as if they were the most precious things in the whole world and Andi found herself wanting to wrap her arms around him.

'I'm ok.' She could feel that there was a slight knick on one finger but didn't want him to let go of her hand anytime soon. She was enjoying the intimate contact with him and a cut on her finger was a small price to pay.

'Are you sure?' he asked, looking at her face, back to her hand and then back to her face, this time, locking his gaze with hers. It was so intense that Andi felt the heat rising in her body and all she wanted to do was kiss him and as much as she was positive, he felt the same, she wouldn't put him in that position.

She nodded. 'It's just a little cut.' Somehow their faces were almost touching, had she moved? Had he? Did it matter? He was so close to her now that she could feel his breath on her lips. Her hand was still held in his. His eyes still searching hers. All she needed to do was just tilt her head a little and they would be kissing.

Andi didn't know if she moved subconsciously or on purpose but suddenly his lips were on hers. So softly, so gently, like being caressed by the wings of a butterfly. Every nerve in her body stood to attention. Of all the kisses she'd received in her life, none had felt like this. Electricity was coursing through her veins and all he'd done was brush his mouth against hers. She resisted the urge to deepen the kiss, stopped herself from putting her arms around him and pulling him close. She longed to weave her hands into his hair, taste him with her tongue but she forced herself to just stay still and let him set the pace.

'I shouldn't have done that.' All to soon it was over, and Andi felt a cold draft blow between them. She looked at Andrew, his face full of sadness. Had the kiss been that bad? If you could even call it a kiss. It had been the briefest of caresses, but my word did she want more.

She placed a reassuring hand on his arm. 'It's ok.'

'But it's not,' he placed his hand over hers. 'There's one thing it isn't and that's ok.'

Andi could tell he was wrestling with himself inside.

'I won't tell anyone,' she promised. 'And it doesn't ever need to happen again.' She dropped her hand from his arm and stepped away from him.

'But I want it to happen again.' He was by her side as quickly as she had moved away. 'I want it to happen over and over again. I want to lay you down on that hay bale over there, strip you naked and kiss every inch of your gorgeous body before making love to you.' He grasped her hands and held them over his heart. 'I want to hear you moan my name as you come, feel your legs wrap round my waist and pull me in deeper.' Andi was at a loss for words. No one had ever spoken to her in this way, and she didn't know if it was the way he was looking at her or the things he was saying but it was one of the most erotic moments of her life.

She could feel how excited she was by his words and longed for him to act on them, she was sure if she made a move, he'd respond but did she want that? Did she want to be the other woman?

'But you're with Carla.' These words had the exact effect she had been hoping for, like pouring water on a fire, his face fell immediately.

'I am,' he spoke sadly. 'And I won't do this to her.' He looked up at Andi. 'Or to you. You deserve so much better than this.' And with those words he turned and was gone.

Chapter 16

By Sunday morning the barn was ready for its first customers and although they weren't officially opening until the following weekend, it seemed silly not to let anyone in and even though they didn't advertise it, the family were pleased to find a few people that visited the shop were excited to go and have a look around and promised to return for the grand opening weekend.

The Pumpkin Patch staff had put their heads together and come up with a variety of ideas to help the weekend go with a bang and since the incident in the barn on Friday, Andi had been keeping herself even busier than before. Her dreams had stepped up a notch since Andrew had kissed her and described what he wanted to do to her and now, every night, she woke up in a pool of sweat, breathing heavily and moaning his name. She couldn't even look at the hay bales, she'd dreamt of them so many times these past few days that when she did, it made her insides do the strangest of things.

'Are you feeling, ok?' Preeti asked later that day.

'Working too hard if you ask me.' Kathy had interrupted. 'And not eating properly either, you look like you've lost weight and your cheeks are sunken.'

It was true, Andi had lost her usual hearty appetite and basically picked at most things, even cake was failing to entice her. Due to having a slightly thin face, losing a few pounds came instantly off her cheeks rather than her thighs where she could afford to lose several inches.

'Looks like sleep isn't going so well either,' Preeti offered. 'You've got bags under your bags.'

'Well thank you both for that wonderful pep talk, I feel so much better now.' Andi snapped, apologising almost immediately. 'I'm just feeling sick all the time and although I'm sleeping, I wake up just as tired if not more so than when I went to bed.'

'You're not pregnant, are you?' Her mum looked at her from the corner of her eye before marching over and standing in front of her.

'No Mum, I'm not pregnant.' Andi had already considered this but thankfully her period had been as regular as clockwork that morning.

'Turn to the side,' Kathy ordered before scrutinising Andi's stomach.

'Mum!' Andi pulled her jumper out of her mum's hands when she went to pull it up. 'I am not pregnant and even if I was, you wouldn't be able to tell yet.' Andi took a large stride away from Kathy and stepped behind the counter. 'I'm just getting a bit sick that's all, usually do this time of year.'

'Lovesick that's what you are.' Dennis butted into the conversation, arriving back in the shop after helping carry a customer's shopping to her car. 'And there's only one cure for that.'

'I am not lovesick,' Andi insisted, knowing full well that she was. Her thoughts constantly whirled around Andrew and what he was doing. Was he thinking about her? 'I've just got a cold coming that's all.' As if to prove this to them she sniffed. 'See.'

'Don't think I didn't see Andrew here the other day,' Dennis admitted much to everyone else's shock, not least of all Kathy who turned on her husband with such a look of astonishment on her face, you'd have thought he'd seen The King roaming around the place.

'And you didn't tell me?' Kathy sounded hurt and angry. 'Why didn't you tell me?'

'Because you'd have pounced on the poor lad.' Dennis suggested. 'He looked like the weight of the world was on his shoulders when he walked out of the barn and the last thing he needed was you being all cheerful and asking him in for tea.'

Kathy went to say something then obviously changed her mind and remained silent.

'He just came into the barn, and I cut my finger.' Andi felt like she now needed to explain.

'And he kissed it better did he?' Dennis accused gently.

'No, don't be silly.' But Andi knew her dad wasn't joking and later on, when it was just the two of them in the storeroom, he confronted her about it.

'I just don't want you getting your heart broken again,' Dennis explained. 'You've just got out of that awful relationship with Drew and its perfectly obvious that as lovely as Andrew seems, he clearly isn't about to finish things with his girlfriend any time soon.'

'But how do you know that?' Andi asked.

'Because he'd have done it already.' Dennis put a comforting hand on her shoulder.

'Maybe he's just waiting for the right moment,' she declared. 'Oh who am I trying to kid,' she shrugged. 'You're right as always.'

Andi spent the next week trying to stop herself thinking about Andrew. Every time she thought about him, she made a conscious effort to push the thought away and by the time Friday came, her daytime hours were becoming less and less obsessed with him and she'd started eating again, having finally lost the sickly feeling in her stomach. Her nights were no better though, and he haunted her dreams constantly.

'Have you tried sleeping tablets?' Chloe suggested as she helped Andi and Fran set the temporary till up in the barn after closing on the Friday. Fran was currently out of earshot, so Chloe had taken the opportunity to quiz her best friend.

'And how exactly will they help?' Andi asked. 'I don't have any problem falling asleep, it is stopping myself dreaming about having sex with Andrew that's the problem.'

'Maybe having sex with someone else could help?' Fran intervened and received looks from the other two. 'You do know that this place echoes and I've heard every word you've been saying.'

Andi was mortified that her sister-in-law knew her dirty secrets.

'You might be on to something there,' Chloe remarked, earning a horrified look from Andi.

'I'm not getting into another relationship so soon after being in one thank you very much.' Andi declared.

'Who said anything about a relationship?' Fran laughed.

'Frances Wilson!' Andi was shocked.

'Oh Andi, grow up,' she teased. 'Are you telling me you've never had a one-night stand before?' Andi shook her head. 'What? Really?' Andi nodded. 'Blimey.'

'I just don't think I could,' she admitted. 'Isn't it dangerous?'

'That's kind of the point,' Chloe answered.

'No, I mean properly dangerous, like psycho killer dangerous.' Andi whispered just in case someone could hear.

'You're not marrying them,' Chloe stated.

'You're just bashing your jiggly bits together.' Fran wobbled her boobs.

'Urgh!' Andi feigned disgust. 'I take it you both have then?'

'On many occasions before I met your brother,' Fran admitted. 'In fact, I think your brother was a one-night stand initially.'

'Really?' Andi was shocked. 'I never knew that.'

'You know I've definitely had a one-night stand or two.' Chloe was smiling at her memories. 'Ok they were with men, but you know.'

'But how do you do it?' Andi couldn't even begin to imagine just having sex with someone and then never seeing them again.

'Do what?' Fran looked at her oddly.

'Just do it.' Andi tried to explain. 'Go up to a complete stranger and ask if they want to have sex with you?'

'That's not really how it works,' Chloe explained. 'You get to know them a bit first, maybe have a dance or a drink if you're in a club.'

'Yeah, you don't just blurt out, hey you, wanna fuck?'

'Frances Wilson!' The three girls turned at the scolding voice of Kathy. 'You kiss my grandson with that mouth.'

'Sorry, Kathy.' Fran looked suitably chastised until Kathy burst out laughing.

'Your face was a picture.' She walked over to them. 'So, who's fucking who?'

'Mum!' Andi had always known her parents to be quite liberal with regards to sex and swearing but just lately she was discovering things about them that she really didn't want to know.

'We were just saying that it might be a good idea for Andi to get back in the saddle so to speak,' Fran offered. 'Maybe a bit of dating would take her mind off Andrew?'

'You know what they say, the best way to get over a man is to get under a new one.' Kathy admitted. 'But I'm still not following where the fucking comes into it?'

As liberal as her mum was, Andi was positive she wouldn't be impressed with the idea of her daughter having sex with random strangers.

'Actually Kathy, we thought a one-night stand would be a good idea!' Andi looked at Chloe with absolute horror on her face.

'Well as long as she uses protection and doesn't go to their house.'

'Mum!' Andi scolded once again. 'I can't believe you just said that.'

'Get in, Mrs Wilson.' Chloe lifted her hand up and Kathy high fived it.

'You're all just a bunch of sexual delinquents.' Andi honestly couldn't believe what she was hearing. She kind of expected it from her best friend and it wasn't totally shocking from her sister-in-law but her mum encouraging her to have a one-night stand was taking things a little too far.

'We could set you up an online dating profile,' Chloe suggested to which Fran readily agreed.

Kathy was nodding eagerly. 'Oh that would be so much fun.'

'Hang on a minute.' Andi wasn't sure why her mum was being so enthusiastic all of a sudden. 'I thought you liked Andrew?'

'I do like him,' Kathy stated. 'But I love you and I can't bear to see you so unhappy.'

'We're not saying a man is the be all and end all.' Chloe coughed at Fran's words. 'Or a woman.' Chloe nodded in satisfaction. 'But Drew has knocked your confidence for six and a few dates with someone new, a bit of how's your father if you're up for it and we'll have the old Andi back before we know it.'

She knew they were right; she had lost some of her spark since being with Drew, she'd tried not to let it affect her but the constant digs and not so subtle comments about her weight and appearance did take a toll on her.

'You are a fine specimen of womanhood and Drew must have been a fool not to realise.' Chloe smiled at Andi. 'And if this bloody Andrew doesn't realise it either then he's an even bigger fool.'

Andi couldn't help it, but tears started falling down her cheeks and she wasn't entirely sure if they were happy or sad or maybe a mixture of both or just a release of emotions.

The four of them crowded in for a group hug before Kathy declared that this wasn't getting anything done and if they wanted the weekend to be a success then they needed to pull their fingers out and get busy.

With men and relationships forgotten, the four women set about adding the finishing touches to the barn before collapsing onto the hay bales where Dennis and Kane found them at almost ten o clock.

'Fish and chips anyone?' Dennis declared, throwing the hot packets into eager hands. The barn was filled with the smell of salt and vinegar accompanied with laughter as everyone sat about and Andi hadn't felt this happy and loved for a long time.

Andrew who? she said to herself, but who was she kidding. He was going to take some getting over.

Chapter 17

Although Andi awoke to torrential rain on the Saturday morning, by the time her and Pumpkin had arrived at the shop it had died off a little and with the barn being undercover they were hopeful people would still visit. A small trickle of customers began arriving around ten and then as the sun came out, more and more people turned up and by the end of the day the Wilson family counted the grand opening as a success.

Pumpkin had been an instant hit but after posing for photo after photo he had decided he'd had enough, and Andi took him to his bed in the storeroom where he snoozed the rest of the afternoon away.

What Andi had enjoyed the most was seeing the look of joy on the children's faces and watching families enjoying time together. Lewis had set up a colouring table, Kane was in charge of the drinks, Kathy and Dennis took turns on the till and in the shop and Andi with Preeti's help in the afternoon, milled around the barn helping the customers and re-stocking if needed. Fran turned up with Matthew dressed in very autumnal dungarees and a pumpkin hat who delighted in toddling about the hay bales with his grandad before falling asleep on the giant pumpkin just as Andi was about to take a picture. The sleeping Matthew however, proved to be even cuter and Andi stored the idea of having the photo enlarged into a poster and placing it in the shop.

As dusk loomed, there were still a few people around, so Kathy lit the candles inside the carved pumpkins and turned on the lanterns and fairy lights that they'd hung around the barn. Of course they could have turned on the strip lighting but the feel in the barn was now magical and the remaining customers appeared reluctant to leave.

'You should open late,' one woman suggested as she lifted her young son out of the wheelbarrow and placed her three pumpkins on the counter. 'It was lovely when we arrived but with the candles and fairy lights on it just takes on a whole different atmosphere.'

They said goodbye to the last group and Dennis followed them down to close the gate after them and take the open sign down. When he arrived back it was to fresh cups of tea and slices of ginger cake that Preeti had brought in from home.

'It's not a bad idea to be fair,' Lewis said, sharing a gingerbread witch with Matthew who was awake once again and hypnotised by the spooky shadows that were being cast on the walls by the candles.

'What? Opening late?' Andi asked to which Lewis nodded.

'I'm happy to stay late a couple of days a week,' Kane said. 'It will only be for a few weeks after all.'

'Naughty Pumpkin.' They all turned at Matthew's baby voice to find Pumpkin at the end of his long lead sitting by Matthew's wellies and tell-tale crumbs on the floor.

'Best keep Pumpkin away from the biscuits in future,' Kathy said, handing Matthew another witch which he immediately handed to Pumpkin much to the husky's delight and Matthew's excited giggle.

'Partners in crime those two,' Fran laughed before becoming distracted by a ping on her phone. 'Back in a minute,' she declared, much to the bewildered looks from everyone else.

'Where's she off to?' Andi asked.

Lewis shrugged his shoulders. 'I haven't got a clue, but she's been so weird since she came home last night. Texting and dashing off upstairs. If I didn't know better, I'd say she was having an affair.'

'Don't be daft.' Kathy took the pumpkin that Matthew offered her and smiled lovingly at her grandson. 'Fran would never do that.'

'I know, Mum, that's what I said.' Lewis held out his hands in confusion. 'But she's definitely up to something.'

The secret stuff with Fran and her phone continued the whole of the next day and Andi was unable to get any information out of her as to what she was up to. Sunday was just as busy as Saturday had been and the barn looked like a tornado had been through it by the time they closed the gate and headed home.

Despite it usually being a day off, Andi was up early on the Monday and dragged a grumpy Pumpkin along with her to the farm shop.

'Don't look at me like that,' she said to him as he reluctantly got in the car. 'I'll grab you some sausages on the way.' This word seemed to perk him up slightly and by the time they had arrived at The Pumpkin Patch, after picking up breakfast, he was slightly more eager and after Andi had chopped up the egg and sausages into his bowl he was once again his normal self.

She grabbed a notebook and started jotting down a list of things that needed doing and got started first on sweeping and tidying up the barn. Pumpkin was on a long lead, a bit like a lead rein for a horse which was attached to a heavy-duty spike in the floor that stopped him from running off. Most of the time he didn't even attempt it but if something caught his eye or nose for that matter, he could bolt, and Andi didn't fancy running after him.

Popping in her Air Pods, she shuffled her Charlie Puth playlist singing along as she brushed the dirty straw and hay into a pile by the door, ready to take to the compost heap later on.

'Er…hello.' A tap on her shoulder accompanied by a male voice made her jump and turn. 'I'm so sorry if I startled you. I did call from the door.' Andi looked over the stranger quickly. He was average looking, average height, average build, in fact everything about him was average. 'Your dog let me in.'

Andi looked at Pumpkin who was sitting at the man's feet. This made her feel safer however as Pumpkin was an excellent judge of character.

'He's a good lad.' She ruffled the dog's ears and Pumpkin, content in a job well done, went back to his makeshift bed, turned around three times before settling back into an instant sleep. 'Can I help you at all?' She took both pods out, popping them in her pocket and pressing pause on her phone.

'The gate was open, but I realised as I got nearer that you're actually closed,' he smiled and suddenly his average face lit up. 'I'll come back tomorrow when you're open.'

'It's ok,' Andi smiled back. 'What was it you wanted?' She had a feeling of recognition suddenly, like she should know who he was but couldn't for the life of her remember. 'Did you need something from the shop?'

'I can't believe you don't recognise me.' So she did know him, or at least he knew her. 'It's Mark, from school.'

'Oh my God, little Mark Ovens?' she hugged him. 'Last time I saw you, you were in shorts and a tank top.'

'Don't remind me,' he shook his head. 'Mum made me wear shorts all through primary school.'

'What happened to you after juniors?' she asked, vaguely recalling that he and a few others never started at the local high school.

'I went to King Henry's.' King Henry the Eighth was the local grammar school.'

'Aren't you the clever one,' she teased.

'Hardly,' he admitted. 'Anyway, how are you?' he asked. 'Married? Kids?' She shook her head.

'Neither I'm afraid.' She tried not to sound sad about this because in all honestly, she wasn't. She knew Drew wasn't the one for her and had she married him, not that he'd asked, she knew she would have been unhappy, and she'd much rather be single and happy than married and miserable. Not that marriage meant misery, but marriage to Drew would have been a nightmare.

'Nor me,' he replied. 'Don't know why we automatically ask that of people do you?' She shook her head. 'It's like its expected of us isn't it. You reach a certain age and then it's all marriage and babies.'

'You're so right,' she agreed. 'We shouldn't be defined by whether or not we're married or have children.'

'Exactly.' He laughed all of a sudden. 'Hark at us putting the world to rights.'

'Do you fancy a drink?' Andi was enjoying his company. 'I can only offer you what we've got in here but if you've got a few minutes, it would be nice to catch up.'

'Sounds good to me,' he said. 'I'm happy to give you a hand, you looked ever so busy when I came in except for the dance moves.'

Andi laughed a little embarrassed. 'Makes it more fun when you're working.' She headed over to the makeshift drinks counter that was set up and switched on the kettle. 'Tea? Coffee?'

'I'd love a nice strong coffee please.' He followed her over. 'So how long have you worked here?'

'It's my family's place.' Mark nodded. 'Dad bought it a few years ago. We thought he was a bit mad but then we all fell in love with it.'

'And do you do this pumpkin thing every year?' he looked around the barn.

'First time,' Andi replied. 'Was opening weekend just gone.'

'Well it looks like it was a success.' She watched as he scanned around. 'Judging by the fact that there's hardly a pumpkin in sight.'

'It was great fun.' Andi hadn't realised until then how empty the shelves actually were and decided they were either going to have to limit opening or buy in more pumpkins because there was no way their small supply was going to last, and they hadn't even got to half term yet.

'It's been all the rage in America for years and it's nice to see it taking off here.' He took the cup of coffee she offered and sipped it straight away. 'Perfect.'

'Doesn't that burn your mouth?' Andi was horrified, she had to wait a good ten minutes for her drink to be at the perfect drinking temperature.

'I think I've got an asbestos throat,' he chuckled, and Andi noticed a little dimple in one of his cheeks.

They spent some hours chatting, and Mark was true to his offer and helped her tidy up the barn, bring in fresh hay and even walked with her and Pumpkin in the field to harvest new stock. She told him of her plans for pumpkins by post to which he expressed huge interest in and wanted to help with the filming.

'I still need to iron out the finer points,' she remarked as they walked back to the barn.

'We could have a practise one evening if you wanted?' Mark suggested. 'I've really enjoyed today,' he said. 'It's been really lovely catching up with you.'

'Me too,' she agreed and was surprised that she actually meant it. 'Why don't you pop by tomorrow?' she suggested, a little shocked at her forwardness.

'Tomorrow it is.' He headed off down the drive with a cheery wave behind him.

'Who was that?' She jumped out of her skin for the second time that day to find her mum and dad in the barn.

'Just an old school friend.' Kathy and Dennis looked at each other knowingly. 'It's not like that.' Andi scolded knowing that it wasn't like that, well, not at the moment anyway. She hadn't asked Mark from a romantic point of view, he wasn't her normal type but it had been nice to spend time with him and she had amazed herself that she hadn't even thought about Andrew all day and was even more amazed when she woke up the next morning and for the first time in ages, she hadn't dreamt of him either.

Chapter 18

The next few weeks were a blur of work, the pumpkin patch barn had taken off like a rocket and the pumpkins by post were proving to be immensely popular too, so much so that as suspected, they had had to limit opening to weekends only and outsource their pumpkin stock from another local farm otherwise they wouldn't have enough for the approaching half term holiday and Andi was adamant she wanted a huge stock. They had made lots of plans and fun activities for the week culminating in a fancy-dress party on the Sunday afternoon with an adult one in the evening.

Andi had seen Mark nearly every day since that Monday and he was proving to be just what she needed for moving on from Drew and her crush on Andrew. She was able to say his name now without feeling as if she'd been kicked in the stomach and she'd be forever grateful to him for opening her eyes to Drew and hoped he was happy.

'So why haven't you kissed him yet?' Fran asked on the Friday evening as they prepared for the upcoming week. The rota had been set and everyone was in every day at some point. They were opening late on the Thursday, Friday and Saturday and the parties were already sold out.

'I want to know the answer to this too?' Chloe had come to help out again after work, but Andi suspected there was more to her sudden enthusiasm for pumpkins than she was letting on.

'It hasn't been the right time.' This wasn't strictly true. There had been many occasions when she'd thought Mark was going to kiss her and she'd panicked and moved away or caused a distraction by saying something or picking up her phone.

'Don't you like him?' Fran's question had been a question that Andi had asked herself a number of times and one to which she could never answer.

'Honestly?' she asked to which Fran and Chloe nodded. 'I don't know.'

'Well that's not very enthusiastic is it,' Chloe stated. 'No sweaty palms? Weak knees?'

Andi shook her head.

'Nothing?' Fran asked, shocked. 'No skipped heart beats?'

'Not even a little flutter,' Andi admitted sadly. 'He's lovely and all that but I just don't think he's for me.'

'Perhaps you're scared,' Chloe suggested.

'Scared? Of what exactly?' Andi looked bemused.

'Scared of moving on maybe,' Fran offered. 'You were with Drew a long time, it's hard to just move on.'

'Trust me,' Andi scoffed. 'I moved on from Drew before I even realised that I had.'

'It's Andrew,' Chloe shouted rather loudly as if the idea had suddenly leapt into her head and needed to be said out loud in case it disappeared as quickly as it had arrived.

'Now you're just being silly.' Andi turned her back to them both and carried on weighing and labelling the pumpkins.

'No, no, hear me out.' Chloe placed a hand on her shoulder and turned her back to face them. 'You're scared to get into a relationship in case Andrew gets wind of it.'

'Nonsense.' Andi wasn't having any of it. 'I was in a relationship when I met him, it's not going to matter if I get in another one. He likes me, I know that, but he doesn't like me enough to end things with his girlfriend.'

'This isn't the same.' Chloe looked to Fran as if she could help her explain but Fran shrugged her shoulders.

'Of course it's the same,' Andi sighed.

'But it isn't,' Chloe continued. 'You made no secret of the fact that you were unhappy with Drew.' Andi nodded. 'But if you started a new relationship, he'd think you don't like him anymore, maybe didn't really like him to start with and then you'd never see him again.'

Andi was loath to admit that Chloe might actually have something in her mad train of thought. She had considered what Andrew would think if he somehow found out that she was dating someone else again so soon after their heart to heart.

'It still doesn't matter though,' Andi concluded. 'He simply doesn't like me enough and that's that so why should I bother what he thinks anymore.' She nodded as if trying to make herself believe in her own words. 'In fact, I'm going to message Mark right now and ask him out and then I'm going to go home and wax every inch of my body, wear some sexy lingerie and fuck his brains out.'

'Well I hope you'll at least take him out for dinner first,' Chloe suggested.

'And maybe wear clothes over the lingerie,' Fran teased before the three of them burst into laughter.

Luckily, Andi had already arranged to meet Mark for a late dinner and after downing a couple of glasses of wine as she got ready, she plucked up the courage to wear a matching red bra and thong. She didn't usually bother with sexy lingerie, what had been the point before, Drew wasn't interested, in fact, he'd made a rather derogatory comment about the size of her arse cheeks when she'd worn a thong before and as she found them highly uncomfortable, like wearing a piece of dental floss, she usually opted for her comfy M&S briefs.

But regardless of whether Mark would see them or not, she put them on, eyed herself in the mirror and was unusually pleased with the view before her. Was she skinny? Not by any stretch of the imagination. She had curves, even some of her curves had curves but she had a good set of boobs, rounded hips and people paid to have a bum like hers.

It was probably the wine talking she said to herself as she scanned her wardrobe and opted for a low cut, body hugging red dress instead of her usual wide legged black trousers and long top.

October was proving to be exceptionally mild this year, so she decided against a coat and slipped into killer heels and when Mark turned up on her doorstep, Andi was pleased to see that his eyes almost popped out of his head, and he appeared lost for words.

She sat as demurely as possible in the front seat and noticed his eyes flicking to her cleavage now and again and smiled to herself. When they reached the restaurant, they were immediately shown to their table and Andi sat facing the other diners because she loved to people watch. Her earlier alcohol confidence was starting to wear off, so she ordered a large glass of red and downed it at once.

'Were you thirsty?' Mark asked, a little concern in his voice.

'I was feeling a bit hot,' she said, fanning herself with the menu as if to emphasise the point.

'I'll say.' Mark caught her gaze with his. 'Did I ever tell you that I was in love with you at school?'

'Were you?' Andi hadn't known this.

'I often thought of you over the years.' He took one of her hands in his. 'I'm so glad we've met up again.' He lifted her hand to his lips and kissed it gently.

'Would you excuse me a minute.' The amount of alcohol consumed on an empty stomach was taking an early effect and she felt like she was about to throw up. She dashed off to the toilet as quickly as she could and bolted herself in one of the stalls.

She heard the door open and a female voice talking on the phone.

'Honestly, Sarah, I think he's going to propose.' Laughter. 'I don't know what I'm going to say.' Pause. 'I know, it's expected isn't it but am I settling?' Agreeing noises. 'He's just so, you know, average.' Another pause. 'You're so right. I can just marry him and then get half of everything down the line.' Agreeing noise. 'That simplified divorce thing makes it so easy. Lilly's came through in just under six months, wasn't it?'

Andi switched off her ears and as the sickly feeling disappeared, took herself out into the sink area where the girl was still on her phone but with a withering look at Andi who realised a few moments later that her boobs were almost falling out, left the toilet with a 'hang on a minute' to her friend.

'What are you doing?' Andi asked her reflection. 'There's a lovely man sitting out there waiting for you, he clearly likes you and you like him.' She stared at herself. '*But you don't fancy him, do you?*' The reflection seemed to ask, and she knew in her heart of hearts that it was never going to work with Mark, she just didn't feel that way about him.

Decision made, she walked out and over to the table, determined to tell him that as nice as he was and as much as she was enjoying their time together, she just couldn't see them as anything other than friends.

Hearing the voice from the toilet made her turn her head to see who the unfortunate soul was that was thinking of proposing to such a cold-hearted bitch. He was currently looking away slightly but she knew instantly that it was Andrew and her heart flipped. Just as she was about to look away, he looked up, as if he knew she was there. His eyes went straight to hers, took in every inch of her in a thorough and swift glance and she felt herself blushing under his gaze even from this distance.

She watched as the girl noticed, followed his gaze and Andi looked away as the girl grabbed his chin and turned him to face her. Andi somehow managed to trip over her own feet and bashed into a chair.

'I am so sorry,' she apologised instantly and looked over at the table again to find the girl smirking and Andrew looking as if he wished he could be anywhere other than there.

'Are you ok?' Mark stood up as she approached. 'You haven't hurt yourself or anything?' He was so full of concern that Andi felt guilty for what she was about to do but in the long run it would be the best thing. She couldn't keep stringing him along, it just wasn't fair to him, and he was too much of a nice guy.

'Listen, Mark.' She was still standing as was he. 'I've been thinking.'

Before she knew what was happening, he'd taken hold of her hands, clasped them against his heart and slapped a kiss upon her lips. She was so shocked that she sat down immediately and looked over to Andrew. His face was one of sadness, as if his whole world had just collapsed around him and she felt like someone had shot an arrow straight through her heart.

'I've been thinking too,' Mark said, clearly not realising her distress. He carried on talking but she didn't hear a word he said as she watched Andrew get up, followed by his girlfriend who shot more daggers at her before they both left the restaurant. 'So what do you think?'

Andi brought her attention back to Mark. 'I'm so sorry, what did you say?'

'I said, I wondered if you'd consider being my girlfriend?'

Chapter 19

'And what did you say to that?' Chloe shouted through the screen on Andi's phone. It was well past midnight and as soon as Mark had dropped her home, she instantly Facetimed her best friend.

'I just told him the truth.' Andi was currently trying to coax a stubborn Pumpkin back in from the garden. He was always like this when she'd gone out and left him for a few hours. The initial excitement of *'oh thank goodness you're home, I missed you'* quickly turned into *'how dare you leave me in this house on my own with nothing but the radio and a gazillion toys for company'*. 'Pumpkin! Will you get in right now!' Pumpkin answered back with a wolfy howl. 'Don't you argue with me my boy! In! Now!' The husky finally did as he was told but not before making out, he was coming in, swerving under the car port for a drink and then as if it was all his own idea, trotting in with his tail up as if he was lord and master.

'That dog gets more like a teenager every day,' Chloe laughed.

'Doesn't he though.' She ruffled his ears as he passed, then closed the door, locking it up and turning off the lights before heading up to bed, Pumpkin closely on her heels. He slept with her every night now, something Andi knew she shouldn't have allowed because he wasn't a small dog by any means and most nights, she woke up on the edge with a husky sized leg in her face.

'So you just came out with it?' Chloe asked as Andi propped the phone on the shelf above the bathroom sink and started brushing her teeth.

'Uh huh,' she nodded with a mouthful of toothpaste. 'I just said he was really nice, but I wasn't ready for a relationship so soon after Drew.'

'So you didn't tell him the truth,' Chloe stated.

Andi rinsed out her mouth and deposited her toothbrush back in the cup. 'Yes, I told him.'

'No, you told him something fabricated to make him feel better.' Andi knew she was right. 'Because let's be honest here, if Andrew turned up on your doorstep right now you wouldn't give a flying fuck how long it had been since you'd split up with Drew.' There was a knock at Andi's door, and she froze, Pumpkin started barking and she looked at Chloe. 'Was that the door?' Andi nodded.

'Who the fuck is that at this time of night?' Pumpkin had already raced down the steps and was standing on guard in front of it.

'Do you think its Andrew?' Chloe looked excited.

'Why would it be Andrew?' Oh she secretly hoped that it was. She was still dressed in her sexy lingerie, had just thrown the dress and shoes off when she'd got home. She could just open the door to him, and he'd walk in, sweep her up in his arms and carry her to the sofa, or maybe they wouldn't even make it that far and they'd just do it in the hallway. Another knock instantly followed by a bark. 'I'll look out the window.'

'Take me with you,' Chloe shouted as Andi went to walk out without her phone but came back instantly and picked it up. 'Jesus, put some clothes on, Andi,' Chloe laughed as she was treated to a bird's eye view of Andi's boobs.

'Oh shut up,' Andi teased. 'You've seen it before.'

'Yes, but whoever is at the door might not have.' Andi grabbed her dressing gown from her bed and walked over to the window. Luckily the streetlights were still on, they went off at one in the morning on Friday and Saturday nights instead of midnight as if that made much of a difference.

'Who is it?' Chloe asked impatiently.

'Will you shut up,' Andi hissed at the phone. 'I haven't even opened the window yet.' Chloe was instantly silent, but Andi placed the phone inside her pocket just to be on the safe side and was rewarded with a muffled oi! She opened the window as quietly and slowly as she could and peered down. It was Andrew standing there and her body filled with emotions it hadn't felt in a long time.

'I can see you; you know,' Andrew called quietly. 'Can I come in; we really need to talk.'

Andi was totally torn, on the one hand she wanted nothing more than to let him in, to sit and talk with him, perhaps he'd finally broken it off with Carla. But then, perhaps she'd broken it off with him and he was here because now he was free and as much as she liked the idea of him being free, she wouldn't be anyone's rebound.

A sound from her pocket made her pull out her phone.

'Who is it?' Chloe asked. 'Is it Andrew?' Andi nodded before sliding the phone back in her pocket and heading downstairs. She quickly checked her face and hair in the hallway mirror, it wasn't great, but it wasn't too bad. She rearranged her bra and resisted the urge to pull the thong out of her bum cheeks for the twentieth time that night.

She quickly ushered the disgruntled Pumpkin into the living room and closed the door behind him so he wouldn't escape. She unlocked the door, pulled it open and stood next to it, leaning as sultrily as she could, one arm above her head on the frame, the other on her hip, pushing the Hufflepuff dressing gown off to one side so most of her body was on show. Granted, the Harry Potter dressing gown wasn't the most alluring of things, but she was a creature of comfort when all said and done and liked nothing more than snuggling in fluffy loungewear with a good film or book.

From the fact that Andrew took one look at her, strode in, and slammed the door behind him, she could have been wearing a bin bag for all that it mattered. He didn't speak, he didn't need to, his face said everything that needed to be said. He swept his arms up inside the dressing gown, and grabbed her shoulders from inside, bringing his lips down to hers with a passion that knocked her off balance for a second before matching it with her own. Her hands went to his shirt, pulling it off him, not caring whether she ripped it, just wanting to feel his skin against hers.

He pushed off the dressing gown, burying his face in between her breasts, a low groan escaping from his mouth before reclaiming her lips for his own. Somehow, his trousers and boxer shorts were down by his ankles and with the swiftest of movements her thong had followed suit.

Andi was against the wall now, her back nudging one of the canvas photos.

'Have you got anything?' she asked breathlessly before he nodded and fumbled quickly for his wallet. This gave Andi a brief moment to catch her breath, to give herself one last talking to. Was this what she wanted? What if he was still with Carla and this was just a booty call? In the end, she decided she didn't care. At this moment she wanted nothing more than to feel him inside of her, all of him. Regrets were for tomorrow, she fully intended to live in the here and now.

He was back as quickly as he had gone, his hands cupping her face as he kissed her as if she were the very air he breathed. Andi had never felt so wanted in her life and it felt so damn good. To know she was having this effect on him, this handsome, sexy man and to be feeling that same desire for him was an earth-shattering experience for her. She'd never had anything like this with anyone else before. To be so consumed with passion for another person that absolutely nothing else mattered in that moment other than to be with them.

Andrew stopped kissing her and with his hands still on her cheeks he looked into her eyes. He seemed to be asking a question and Andi knew exactly what that question was, and she nodded her agreement before he hoisted her up onto his hips and thrust into her. She had never come so quickly and with such pleasure that she didn't want it to end. Stars prickled under her eyes, and she arched her back as he cupped her shoulders with his hands and pushed her harder down on to him.

Wave after wave engulfed her as he kept up the rhythmic movement, never faltering once, hitting her spot over and over again, running his tongue over her breasts, nuzzling the hollow of her neck. Just when she thought she couldn't take any more he moved her bra away with his mouth and took one of her nipples inside and she felt like she would burst.

'Andrew,' she moaned into his ear, digging her nails into his back, and wriggling slightly. She knew that this had tipped him over the edge almost instantly. His control slipped immediately, and his thrusts became deeper and harder, and he cried out as his whole body went rigid then shuddered slightly as his passion abated.

The pair of them stayed there for what felt like an eternity. Andi didn't want to move, not ever. She wanted to stay there, locked in his embrace, his head resting on her chest, all of him inside of her. She didn't want to speak, didn't want to break the moment. But nature was having none of it and she felt him slip away. She hoped Andrew wasn't slipping away at the same time.

She slowly slid back to the floor and now that her eyes were level with his, she could see that she needn't have worried. He was smiling at her, a mixture of pleasured shock, but not the smallest hint of guilt or regret.

'Wow!' he said, his smile taking over his whole face. 'I didn't know it could be like that.'

'Nor me,' she kissed the tip of his nose. 'We've clearly been doing it with the wrong people.' She instantly regrated her choice of words and looked to the floor.

'It's ok.' He placed a finger under her chin and lifted her face to his. 'I finished with her. She's not the one for me, I know that now, I've known that for a long time, even before I met you but meeting you made me see it. Losing you made me see it.' He kissed her again, this time it was long and deep and full of love. 'I was all set to ask her to marry me, but then I saw you with that chap and it broke my heart. I know you'd been with Drew all this time, but I never saw the two of you together and then when he kissed you, I saw red. I wanted to punch his lights out.'

'I thought you were disgusted with me for being with someone new.' Andrew shook his head.

'It was just what I needed, a wake-up call if you like.' He kissed her again. 'Like I said that day, I can't be without you Andi.'

'Well now you don't have to be.' She threw her arms around him and then giggled as the cold condom touched her leg.

'I'd best get rid of this,' he smiled cheekily. 'Upstairs?'

'First door on the left,' she pointed and watched his naked backside wiggle up the stairs because he still had his shoes on and his clothes around his ankles. She bent down and picked up her dressing gown, sliding her arms inside before retrieving her discarded thong from the corner of the mirror and smiled to herself.

'Well that was a turn up for the books.' Andi stopped dead in her tracks before realising that Chloe had seen everything.

Chapter 20

'I'm down here you nitwit.' Andi looked in horror as she saw her phone, Chloe's face still on it leaning up against the wall, directly opposite where her and Andrew had just been. 'He's got a nice arse I'll give him that. Made me think about batting for the other side I can tell you.'

'Chloe Louise Masterson!' Andi scolded. 'You did not just watch me and Andrew having sex?'

'Oh don't get your knickers in a twist,' she giggled. 'Not that you've got any knickers on.' She giggled again at her own joke. 'It isn't the first time my dear.'

'What on earth do you mean by that?' Andi tied the dressing gown belt around her and headed into the kitchen to be met with a moody stare from Pumpkin who had taken himself off to his bed.

'I know what you and Gregory Parker were up to in that sleeping bag at his 18th birthday party.' She mocked hugging and kissing herself. 'I've heard quieter elephants.'

'You never said.' Andi was mortified by this.

'Why would I?' Chloe shrugged. 'You told me the next morning anyway.'

'Jesus Chloe,' Andi scolded kindly. 'I know you're my best friend, but you really don't need to know everything about me.'

'Yes, I do.' Chloe confirmed to which Andi nodded her agreement. 'How else can I guide you through this perilous journey of life if I don't know?'

'True.' Andi's thoughts went back to what had just happened and a goofy smile spread over her face.

'Alright you, get on upstairs and make love to that man like your very life depends on it.' Andi blew Chloe a kiss and switched off her phone, checking it three times before deciding to leave it downstairs as well, just in case.

'Good morning sleepyhead.' Andi opened one eye and then another very slowly. She felt completely disorientated by the voice that was speaking to her. Her body ached all over as if she'd done a massive work out at the gym, well she imagined it would feel like this after never having actually been inside one. She felt utterly exhausted as if she'd been awake half the night and then realisation dawned on her, and the goofy grin came over her face yet again. 'Now that's a look I could get used to seeing every morning.'

'I'm just glad you're still here.' Andi scooched herself up in the bed, realised she was naked and pulled the duvet up to her neck in embarrassment.

'It's a little late for that don't you think?' Andrew wiggled his eyebrows suggestively before crawling seductively on the bed. 'I've seen every inch of this gorgeous body.' He flung back the cover. 'And now I intend to spend all day kissing every inch of it too.' Andi squealed in delight as true to his word, he kissed her toes and her foot, up one leg, stopping tantalising close to her womanhood, before starting again on the other side, but this time the kisses edged closer and closer.

He teased her with a kiss on one side, then moving to the other, each time getting lower and lower until he was hovering, millimetres above. She could feel his breath and she squirmed, trying to close her legs but he shook his head and tutted, pressing his hands against her thighs before exploring her with his tongue.

'Fucking hell!' She screamed and dug her hands into the bed sheet, writhing in the ecstasy he was giving. Just as she thought she couldn't take anymore he stopped.

'Was that the door?' he looked up at her.

'Why would it be the door?' She asked, panting heavily, and wishing he'd just get back to the matter in hand but not feeling she knew him well enough to just shove her hand behind his head and push him back down there.

'I'm sure I heard the door.' Andrew lifted himself up on his hands.

'It was probably the neighbours,' Andi said. 'They do like to slam about a bit.'

Andrew shrugged, lowered his head once more and instantly Andi was back in the zone. It had never been like this with Drew, on the rare occasions when she had been about to climax, if he stopped or moved, she could never get back to the spot again but with Andrew, it was so different, and she now knew what it meant to be with the right person.

She moaned, biting her lip as she weaved her hands into his hair and spread her legs open as far as she could to allow him to plunge even deeper.

'Is everything ok, Andi? It's just you didn't come into work and you're not answering your phone and OH MY GOD!' The door closed as quickly as it had opened. 'I'm so sorry, I'll let myself out, pretend I wasn't here.' Kathy's voice trailed away along with her footsteps as Andi and Andrew stared at each other.

'Oh Jesus Christ.' Andrew sat on the edge of the bed. 'I told you I heard the door.'

Andi put her head in her hands, undecided whether to burst into laughter at the absurdity of the situation or crawl under the duvet and never come out after being found spread eagled on the bed while your new boyfriend who your parents didn't even know was your new boyfriend in fact, could she even call him her boyfriend, was doing wonderous things with his tongue.

The word boyfriend sat rather nicely in her head, and she decided to try and make light of the situation.

'Just be grateful it wasn't my dad.' This had completely the opposite effect to the one she had intended, and Andrew shot up.

'I need to go and apologise,' he said, walking towards the door. 'What must your mum think of me? She didn't even know we were together and here I am, taking advantage of her daughter.'

'I'd hardly call it taking advantage. I seem to remember being a more than willing volunteer if not the driving force behind some of it.' Andi couldn't believe how calm she was feeling about it. Granted, it would have been a very different story had it been her dad, but she knew her mum would keep it to herself and make up some other story as to why she wasn't in work, at least she hoped her mum would. She bit her lip, slightly worried by the story her mum would actually tell but determined to calm Andrew down. 'In fact, I can distinctively recall the reverse cowboy was somewhat new to you.' She hoped this memory might ease him a little, it was certainly making her hotter and she couldn't wait to try it out again.

'It's no good Andi,' he opened the door. 'I'll have to drive there right now and throw myself on her mercy.'

'You'd best put some clothes on first,' she giggled at the sight of him standing butt naked in the doorway. 'And if you want to throw yourself on someone, how about throwing yourself over here at me.' She was shocked by her own brazenness and sudden surge of confidence. Chloe had been right all along; it was just being with someone that gave in the bedroom department just as much as they took that made all the difference. Andi had found herself in positions she wouldn't have dreamt of doing with Drew, not in a million years. Yet with Andrew, she'd been spread eagled, on top, underneath and even at one point, she still didn't know how, was sideways and upside down both at the same time.

'But Andi, I won't be able to look them in the eye again.' She could see her words had made him hesitate.

'Mum won't say anything.' She slid sexily off the bed and knelt in front of him, smiling to herself when she saw him go hard instantly. 'She'll just be overjoyed that we're together.' She looked up at him from her position and licked her lips slowly, pleased to see that his face took on an almost pained expression, like he was battling with himself over what to do.

Andi flicked out her tongue just a little and touched the very tip of his penis and was rewarded with a sharp intake of breath from Andrew. Next, she ran her tongue all the way down and back up again, so slowly and deliberately that he had to brace himself against the wall and she knew then that she had him totally under her control. With just a slight touch of her hand, she guided him into her mouth and felt him come almost instantly.

'Fucking hell, Andi,' he shuddered with his orgasm. 'Where the hell have you been all my life?' He lowered himself down to her level and gently eased her to the floor before finishing what he had started a few moments ago when they had been so rudely interrupted.

'I've been here all along,' she said, kissing him on the nose after her own climax had calmed. 'We just hadn't met each other.'

'Thank goodness Pumpkin chased after that squirrel.' Andrew lay back on the floor beside her, his hands resting easily on his stomach. 'We'd never have met otherwise.'

'Oh, I think we would.' She turned on her side and started running a finger round one of his nipples. 'There's no way either of us was meant to be with our previous partners. The universe would have had us meet at some point or another, I'm sure of it.'

He took hold of her hand and lifted it to his lips, placing a soft kiss in her palm before clasping it against his chest. 'I've still got to face your mum though.' But this time he laughed at his words and Andi joined him.

Chapter 21

'I honestly don't know what to say, Mum, it's just been the best weekend ever.' Andi had come in extra early on the Monday morning to make up for the fact that she'd been noticeably absent all weekend. She'd felt incredibly guilty for leaving everyone on what had turned out to be one of their busiest weekends since the shop opened. But as her mum had told everyone that Andi was unable to get out of bed and was utterly exhausted from some virus called Andrenitus, (her mum had been particularly pleased with this name and had attached no less than ten laughing emojis on her text informing Andi of what she had told everyone), Andi had had no choice but to stay home.

Not that she had wanted to be anywhere else and as she had in fact, spent most of the time in bed, Kathy wasn't technically lying. Andi had never felt so sexually content in all her life. In her wildest dreams, she had never imagined the positions that her and Andrew had gotten into, the places his hands and tongue could reach and the amount of intense pleasure he could give and she in return. It had never been like that with anyone.

Giving such pleasure to Andrew was as satisfying to Andi as when she was on the receiving end. It gave her such confidence to know that with a slight flick of her tongue at the perfect moment or a tiny increase in pressure could cause him to spiral out of control.

Sex in the shower had been another new experience and one she was looking forward to repeating often. The heat of the water only added to the sensuality and Andrew looked even hotter wet.

It had been an awkward first meeting with her mum after the interruption on Saturday but Kathy as usual took it all in her stride and just hugged Andi, told her she hadn't seen anything other than Andrew's very nice arse and had immediately averted her eyes. Although Andi knew this wasn't strictly true because she could remember with acute deliciousness the exact position they had been in at the time, she was grateful to her mum for pretending.

'You walked into the shop this morning and it was as if you were floating.' Kathy remarked. 'The way you held yourself, that little smile you had on your face was just so wonderful. I'm so pleased you've found each other.'

'I do feel bad for Mark, though.' Andi had been riddled with feelings of guilt.

'Well, you can blame Fran and Chloe for that.' Kathy crossed her arms in angrily. 'Meddling in other people's love lives. It only causes trouble.'

'What do you mean?' Andi asked. 'What on earth has it got to do with Fran and Chloe?'

'They set you up a dating profile on Fran's phone.' Kathy didn't need asking twice. 'And Chloe recognised Mark from school. Honestly those two. I've a good mind to knock their heads together.'

'They meant well,' Andi smiled; she didn't think she had any other emotion in her at the moment other than sheer happiness. 'And at least we know now why Fran was being so weird with her phone.'

'That's true I suppose.' Kathy stood up and arched her back with a groan.

'Are you ok, Mum?' Andi asked concerned.

'I'm fine, love,' Kathy replied. 'Just twisted my back a little in the night.'

Andi nodded. 'Did you sleep funny? I'm always doing that, especially now Pumpkin shares the bed with me. I wake up on the edge and he's spread eagled in the middle.'

'Well it was me that was spread eagled.' Kathy laughed. 'Honestly the positions your dad can get me in.' She shook her head with a huge grin on her face. 'Do you know last night we did…'

Andi stood up and placed a hand gently over her mum's mouth. 'TMI Mum, TMI!'

'How is the most beautiful girl in the world?' Andi turned at the familiar voice that had entered the back of the shop.

'On top of the world.' She almost ran to him and kissed him hard as if they'd been away from each other for weeks and not just a few hours. 'I thought you were busy today?'

'I am extremely busy, but it appears that I can't concentrate on anything other than the thought of your naked body up against mine.' Andi could feel this was true even through his jeans and hers. 'Do you fancy a walk?'

'That would be lovely,' she grabbed her coat. 'I'll just fetch Pumpkin from the barn.'

'As much as I love the ginger rascal, can we leave him here?' he asked, a knowing glint in his eye.

'I suppose we could just sneak out the back.' Andi felt a frisson of excitement as Andrew ran a hand over her bum. 'Dad's in the shop and Mum and Preeti are in the barn.' Andrew's hand was now inside the waist band of her jeans, and she couldn't think straight. 'Just going on my break Dad.' She called into the shop and without waiting for an answer, yanked Andrew out of the back door and onto the field.

It was full of people, and it took them a long time to reach the sanctuary of the wooded area that stood at the end. Dressed in her uniform, Andi was inundated with questions and requests for help and as much as she wanted to tell them all to find someone else, she knew she couldn't and ended up helping everyone that she could, even Andrew went to the aid of a family who were in need of assistance when their trolley truck became stuck in the mud.

'Finally,' he said, grabbing her hand and pulling her deeper into the woods before slamming her against an Oak tree in his desire and need for her. 'I've been dreaming of this since we got dressed this morning.'

His hands were inside her shirt, cupping her breasts, caressing each nipple till it was taut and crying out for his tongue but this was otherwise engaged exploring every inch of her mouth. Her fingers weaved in his hair, pulling him as close to her as he could be, wanting to crawl under his skin and be a part of him forever.

It wasn't long before her trousers and pants were round her ankles and he was thrusting inside of her. This was no time for long patient love making. They both needed each other at this very moment. Andi could feel the bark rubbing against her back and she was grateful of the thick fleece she had thought to put on, then all thoughts shot out of her head as Andrew's mouth sucked on her breast and she felt herself reach that wonderful height of ecstasy that up until this weekend had been lost to her.

Despite it only having been a few hours since they had made love and after an arduous weekend of unbridled passion, Andi came quickly and ferociously with an intensity that shocked her to her very core. She shuddered over and over as wave after wave engulfed her and she longed for it to never end.

Collapsing onto his shoulder once she felt him finish, Andi couldn't help it, but she cried. Huge fat globs of tears fell down her cheek and she sobbed.

'I'm so sorry,' she said, sliding down the tree so her feet once again touched the ground.

'It's me that should be saying sorry.' Andrew looked pained. 'Did I hurt you?' He started to pull her clothing up and inspected her for damage.

'No.' She knew he didn't believe her. 'No,' she said more forcefully this time, cupping his face in her hands and kissing him gently. 'I'm just happy.' She made one of those snort cry sounds and then laughed. 'I sound like Dawn French in the Vicar of Dibley when Richard Armitage proposes to her.'

'I've never done it against a tree before.' He took his condom off carefully and wrapped it in some tissue. 'It's much more glamorous in films, isn't it? I'm going to have to walk with this in my pocket now.' They laughed together and it felt so good, so right. 'We'd best head back before your dad wonders where you are.'

'Let's just stay here for a while.' She pulled him back into her embrace. 'I can't imagine a more peaceful place than right here, right now.'

They both leaned against the tree, looking up at the autumn sunshine filtering through the leaves that were nearing the end of their time on the tree. Soon they would fall, lining the floor with their orange and red carpet. A buzzing in Andrew's pocket made him sigh and he pulled out his phone reluctantly.

'I need to go.' He kissed her gently on the tip of the nose. 'Meeting a new client at 2 and I think I might need a quick spruce and change of clothes before I do.' Andi hadn't noticed that the knees on his jeans were streaked with green moss stains from the tree.

'Yes, that might be a good idea,' she giggled as she pulled a leaf out of his hair.

'You can talk.' He mirrored the gesture on her, taking three leaves and a little piece of bark from her ponytail.

'I don't think I've ever been this happy in my entire life.' They walked hand in hand back towards the shop, Andrew leaving her on the field with customers with a wink and a squeeze of the hand and in that squeeze was the promise of a future.

Chapter 22

It was the end of the day and Andi was still smiling. She'd had thoughts and memories of Andrew throughout the afternoon which made her blush from ear to ear and her mum and Preeti had exchanged knowing glances. How was it possible for one person to feel all this joy in such a short time. When Fran had arrived for her shift after lunch, she had immediately apologised to Andi for the dating profile and promised never to interfere again although was happy to take part of the credit that at least one good thing had come out of it and finally she could be happy with Andrew.

'I think that's everyone,' Dennis announced, coming through the barn door around half past four.

'Are you sure?' Fran asked. 'I'm positive there was a woman and a toddler who came in a while ago, but I haven't seen them leave yet.'

'I'll check the baby changing room. The door has a nasty habit of sticking,' Kathy announced, leaving the others to start tidying and cashing up. There wasn't a lot of cash these days, post COVID most people used cards now, so this process had become much less time consuming. It was a good ten minutes later before Kathy arrived back in the barn with a tear-stained boy of around three in her arms and a disgruntled looking woman staggering behind in heels. 'Can

we get a nice biscuit and a cup of coffee for mum please?'
Kathy asked as soon as they arrived.

'I'd rather have a latte, and do you have soya milk?' The
woman asked before brushing imaginary dirt from one of the
tables and plonking herself down. 'We've been locked in
that room for ages. I've a good mind to make a complaint to
the council.'

Andi who had been busy restocking the pumpkins turned to
look at the woman and her face fell instantly. It was none
other than Andrew's girlfriend Carla. Ex girlfriend she
reminded herself then also reminded herself that this ex
knew who she was. What if Andrew had told Carla that he
was in love with Andi? She'd best try and sneak out.

'Andi?' Too late, her mum had seen her. 'Grab some soya
milk from the shop will you please.'

'Yes, Mum.' She needn't have worried. Carla looked straight
at her with absolutely no recognition in her face whatsoever.
Andi knew she'd been dressed up when she'd seen her at the
restaurant but was she surely that unrecognisable? She stole
a glance at herself in the shop door as she passed through
and was more than pleased with her reflection. Perhaps
Carla's nose was so far up in the air that she didn't actually
see anyone else.

'Here you go, Sweetie.' Andi returned to find the toddler
was now fully engaging with Dennis at the colouring table
and her mum handing him a biscuit. Pumpkin was asleep, the
drama of the moment had not been enough to cause more
than a quick look through half opened eyes before snuggling
his nose back under his tail.

'You should mark that room as out of order.' Carla was still annoyed. 'Or at least put a warning on the door. We could have been locked in there for hours, all night even. What if you hadn't heard me banging? And don't get me started on the faulty tap. I'm soaked through.' This was when Andi noticed she was wearing a Pumpkin Patch jacket, hers if she wasn't mistaken.

'We can only apologise,' Preeti assured.

'I'll get them both fixed first thing in the morning,' Dennis apologised.

'Why don't you come back tomorrow and have a pumpkin hunt on us?' Kathy suggested much to Andi's despair. 'Andi and Pumpkin will take you both round the field and the little man can have a ride in one of the trucks.' Carla's face looked a little interested at this.

'We'll throw in a fifty-pound gift card for the shop as well.' Andi couldn't believe her parents.

'Make it a hundred and I won't go to the newspapers.' Andi couldn't believe the cheek of her or at how swiftly her father agreed.

'You've got a deal.'

'Do you know who that was?' Andi said to them after a collective sigh of relief had been released once Carla had eventually left with the boy who they had discovered was called Kai. The others shook their heads and shrugged shoulders and Andi wondered why she'd phrased it that way, of course they wouldn't know who she was. 'It's Andrew's ex, Carla.'

'Well no wonder he finished with her. What a hateful young woman,' Preeti observed.

'He never mentioned that she had a son,' Andi pondered.

'Probably never came up in conversation.' Kathy tidied the colouring away, putting the crayons in their pot with a satisfying plonk. 'They didn't seem particularly close, perhaps Kai lives with his dad? Perhaps she's not his mum?'

'I definitely heard her call him Mum,' Fran stated to which Dennis agreed.

'All I know is that we've got to put up with her tomorrow.' Andi's week had taken a turn for the worse. 'What if she recognises me from the restaurant? What if Andrew has told her about me?'

'She would have said if she recognised you.' Her dad placed a comforting arm around her shoulders. 'And what does it matter if she does?'

'Because if she does…' Andi realised all of a sudden why her parents had been so accommodating with Carla. 'And Andrew has cited me as a reason for their breakup, then she could make things very difficult for us indeed.'

Her parents' faces fell along with that of Preeti and Fran.

'Then you'd best stay out of her way tomorrow as much as possible.' Dennis said decisively. 'Your mother and I will do the pumpkin hunt with her. You can stay in the barn, and we'll serve her in the shop.'

Andi was instantly relieved that she wouldn't have to spend any more time with Carla but all the way home she agonised over telling Andrew about the encounter with her. In the end she decided against it and put all thoughts of Carla out of her mind.

Pumpkin had been fed at the farm, so she jumped into the shower as soon as she got back, deliberating over and over on whether to get dressed, dress sexy or just to open the door to him in nothing but her birthday suit. The evening was already chilly, and the first frost of the season had been predicted so she opted for her Hufflepuff onesie with nothing on underneath. At least this way she would be warm and comfy until Andrew arrived but could be naked in seconds.

Just the thought of him arriving was making her stomach do flip flops and her heart beat faster. She'd not long got dried but as she anticipated the night ahead, she was soon wet again and reached for her phone to check the time. It was almost seven. They hadn't said a time but after today's events in the woods she thought he'd have been here by now.

Switching on the TV, she put the second season of Bridgerton on again to enjoy Anthony and Kate's romance once more. Two episodes in and she was starting to worry, by the end of the third episode, not even their almost kiss in the garden after Kate is stung by a bee was enough to distract her and she sent off another text, followed by a phone call.

By eleven there was still no answer, so she decided to get dressed and drive to his house and then remembered that she hadn't a clue where he lived so she started pacing.

'Something has happened to him,' she said to the screen as soon as Chloe answered the video call.

'Right, calm down and tell me what's going on.' Andi tried to relax but she was completely on edge and continuing her pacing. 'I'm coming over.' Chloe said just as a knock came on the door. 'See, worrying about nothing. Now, I'm off to bed, got an early start in the morning.'

Andi blew a kiss, ended the call, and threw caution to the wind. She unzipped her onesie and slipped out of it before pulling open the door.

'Come on then Big Boy and show me what I've been missing.'

'Andi! Really!' Drew's voice chilled her to the bone, and she tried to cover herself with her hands, not an easy task with double D boobs. She shot away from the door and grabbed her winter coat that was hanging up, zipping it right up to the neck so she looked like an eskimo.

'What on earth are you doing here?' She had forgotten to shut the door, so Drew had stepped inside and closed it behind him. 'You need to leave right now.'

'I came to see if we could work things out but obviously you've moved on already.' He looked at her as if he could see right through the coat. 'Who on earth were you expecting to answer the door? And why don't you have any clothes on?'

'Not that it is any of your business, but I was expecting my new boyfriend and the reason I didn't have any clothes on was because as soon as he gets here, I'm going to fuck his brains out.' It felt good to talk to Drew this way. Even if she was feeling slightly deflated from Andrew's absence and a little shocked by Drew's sudden appearance, she wasn't about to show it in front of him. 'In fact, it's all we've done the entire weekend.' She was glad to see him squirm slightly. 'We've fucked in the bed, on the floor and up the wall. We've shagged in the shower and the living room, and he even bent me over the dining room table, and we did it doggy style before tea.'

'You've become a right little slut haven't you,' he spat, but this would be insult only made Andi feel more powerful.

'If being a slut means feeling desired and wanted and giving and receiving sexual attention equally then I'd rather be a slut than a stunted prude any day and I'd be grateful if you'd get out of my house and never come back.'

Chapter 23

'You said what?' She had rung Chloe on her way into work and was chatting over the car's blue tooth system. 'Oh you go girl, I bet his face was a picture.'

'I've never seen him so angry Chlo.' This felt like an understatement to Andi. Drew's face had become twisted and ugly in seconds. The veins in his neck had seemed to pop and his cheeks had gone a deep shade of scarlet. 'It scared me a little, but I didn't let him see that. I just stood my ground and insisted he leave the house. Poor old Pumpkin was going mental in the kitchen. Growling and snarling at the door, I've never heard him like that.'

'He'll have wanted to protect you, good job he couldn't get to Drew to be honest,' Chloe replied.

'You're telling me.' Andi had been extremely grateful that she'd put Pumpkin behind a closed door, although incredibly soft and docile he was unwaveringly loyal to Andi and thirty kilos of angry husky was not an easy thing to control.

'Still nothing from Andrew?' Chloe's tone was hopeful.

'Nothing at all.' Andi was parked now and could see she was the first in, probably because she'd hardly slept. 'I'm really worried about him. I've phoned and texted, but they've not even been delivered.'

'Maybe he lost his phone or something daft like that.' Andi wasn't convinced by Chloe's answer. 'These things do happen you know.' Andi laughed. 'Well, to me they do.'

'I'd best go.' She switched off her engine. 'Speak to you in a bit.'

'Don't worry Andi, he'll turn up,' Chloe reassured. 'Love you.'

Andi wasn't comforted by Chloe's words in the slightest and with Pumpkin beside her she trudged to the shop, unlocking the padlock, and pulling up the shutter. It was rare that she arrived this early and it always scared her a little to be in the shop when it was empty and still dark outside. She switched on the light and headed to the back to settle Pumpkin and get the kettle on.

Car headlights made her look out and she felt instantly calmer knowing her parents had arrived. She called 'Good Morning' as the little bell above the door tinkled.

'Good morning yourself.' She felt arms reach around her from behind and knew instantly that it was Andrew. She turned in his embrace, plastering his face with kisses before remembering how incredibly worried she'd been.

'My God Andrew, where the hell have you been?' she smacked him on the chest, a little harder than she had intended.

'I lost my phone, no idea where it is and when I got home last night, Carla turned up on my doorstep absolutely distraught. I had no way of contacting you, wouldn't even know if you had a landline, don't have your email and although I considered driving to your house at two o clock this morning I didn't think you'd appreciate that and then when I did drive to your house you weren't there so I hoped against hope that you were here and here you are.' He'd rattled off the words so quickly that Andi was positive he wasn't lying. His face looked sorry and upset and the tone of his voice was sincere. Her ears had picked up instantly on Carla's name and the two in the morning part.

'Was Carla there a while then?' she asked.

'She wouldn't leave.' Andi felt his arms weave around her back. 'She kept babbling on about being locked in some shop toilet and suing the shop for compensation.'

'She'd better bloody not!' Andi said, anger rising inside. 'She said she wouldn't. Oh that woman is a piece of work.'

'Andi?' Andrew was looking at her with a quizzical expression. 'What's going on?' Andi explained all about the previous afternoon and how they were having to placate her today. 'I'm sorry for that.'

'You don't need to apologise for her,' Andi explained, realising that this was exactly what she used to do for Drew. 'She isn't your responsibility.

'I know, it's just…' he paused. 'I feel sort of responsible. I mentioned about this place and all the lovely things you had going on so she must have decided to bring Kai here.'

Andi was just about to press him further about Kai when her parents arrived, calling rather loudly as they walked in.

'That will be their tactful entrance after what happened with Mum the other day.' Andi watched Andrew's face turn a bright red. 'She's fine about it, honestly.'

'I know, but just the thought if it makes me go all funny,' he shivered.

'The thought of it makes me go all funny too.' Andi winked at him and ran a suggestive hand down his chest. 'I was very much looking forward to a repeat performance last night you know.'

'Oh were you indeed,' he grinned at her. 'Perhaps we could meet in the woods for lunch.' His mouth was hovering above hers.

'Sounds like a date to me.' She stood up on her tip toes and captured his lips in a quick kiss just before her parents walked in the back.

Andrew arrived a little after twelve carrying a rather large paper bag from Books and Brews. They'd all been rushed off their feet and Andi was desperate for a break. Preeti and Kane had arrived for their afternoon shifts and lunch time cover so while her parents headed home for a quick sandwich, Andi, Andrew, and Pumpkin took off for a walk.

It was a glorious autumn day, dry and slightly chilly due to the bright but weak sun in the sky. Andi was glad she had her burnt orange jumper and fur lined boots on. They held hands as they moved towards the woods, Pumpkin chasing and sniffing the leaves that they kicked as they walked. They could see people in the pumpkin field, choosing pumpkins, posing for selfies, and generally having fun, it made Andi smile. She couldn't remember a time where she'd felt more content.

Andrew's hand was warm in hers and she felt safe. Safe in the knowledge that he would never intentionally hurt her, that wherever this was going, whether it be long or short term, she hoped it would be very long term, that they were two adults on the same wavelength, both emotionally and physically. That they respected each other and would at all times consider the other's feelings.

'Well I'll be damned.' Andrew bent down as they approached the tree they had kissed under the day before and placed the bag on the floor. 'There's my phone.' He waggled it at her, and it lit up briefly showing his lock screen. Andi couldn't be sure, but she was positive it was Carla and Kai. 'I blame you.' He threw his arms around her and kissed her. Andi couldn't help herself, but she stiffened. 'What's the matter?' His arms dropped away from her.

'I'm being silly,' she replied.

'I'll be the judge of that,' he said. 'If we're going to make this work, then I don't want you hiding anything from me.'

'Who's Kai?' There didn't seem to be any point in beating around the bush, so she just came out with it.

Andrew looked at her. 'I told you, he's Carla's son.'

'But what is he to you?' she pressed. 'Why do you have them on your phone?'

'Do I?' he looked genuinely surprised at this and pulled out his phone again. 'Hadn't even realised to be fair. As soon as I look at the screen it just opens. I'll change it now.'

Did she ask again? She was starting to sound like a fishwife, but she couldn't help it. 'Doesn't he live with her?' She tried a slightly different tactic.

'With Carla?' he laughed as he faffed with buttons on his phone. 'That would throw a spanner in the works and no mistake.'

'What on earth do you mean?' Andi couldn't imagine being a mother and not wanting to be with your children all the time.

'She isn't the motherly type shall we say. He lives with his dad most of the time and just comes and visits Carla once or twice a year. I think I've only met him a handful of times.' *So why have a photo of him on your phone?* She was desperate to ask but felt this was prying way too much, luckily, he answered. 'Carla put this on, she likes people to think she's mother of the year. Plus it's from a professional photo shoot so she "allows" this one to be out in the open.' He held his phone up in front of her. 'Say pumpkins.'

Andi posed quickly. 'I didn't think much of her to be fair when I met her.'

'She's not the politest of people at the best of times so I dread to think what she was like after being locked in the loo for two hours.' He held up his phone where there was now a smiling photo of her. 'Better?

'Much!' she smiled and shivered slightly as a cold breeze drifted past. 'And she'd best bring my jacket when she comes back today.'

'Was she really that bad? Hold on a minute.' Andrew shot his hands up in the air. 'Let's have lunch while you tell me again.'

Andrew spread out the blanket that they'd brought with them, and Andi explained the events of the previous afternoon once more as they tucked into sandwiches and cakes. Pumpkin had curled himself up and was now fast asleep after eating ham and cheese and snaffling half of a mini sponge cake that Andrew had rather foolishly placed within sniffing distance.

'She was horrible Andrew, just a spiteful, stuck-up cow,' Andrew laughed at her.

'That's one way to describe her.' He started putting the wrappers back into the bag. 'I'd love to of seen her face though when your parents got the door open. And she definitely didn't recognise you?'

'If she did, she didn't say.' Andi picked up the last bit of scone and popped it in her mouth. 'But let's face it, I looked vastly different that night to my usual attire.'

'You're doing it again,' he scolded. 'Putting yourself down.'

'Can't help it,' she shrugged. 'I'm so used to insults disguised as compliments that I end up beating myself up as well.'

Andrew pushed himself onto his hands and knees and slowly positioned his legs, so they were either side of her outstretched ones. She was leaning back on her hands, her elbows behind her as he moved his face closer to hers.

'Well now you have me, and I don't intend to give you anything other than full blown compliments.' He kissed her quickly. 'I happen to think you look amazing in absolutely everything you wear whether it be dressed up to the nines in your Sunday Best or in your work clothes.' He kissed her again. 'And I haven't seen you naked enough yet to form an opinion so let's get that rectified as soon as possible.' He pushed her gently down onto the blanket, his body falling easily to the side of hers.

Andi felt like a teenager again, making out in the local park with Gregory. She felt shy and awkward with Andrew as she had done back then. Even though they'd already had sex multiple times and seen and sucked each other's wobbly bits, this felt like it was on another level, that their relationship was starting to take off.

She knew she was falling for him, had fallen for him if she was perfectly honest and scolded herself for failing to protect her heart after its beating from Drew. She knew, no, hoped Andrew was different, that she could trust his words and his oh so sexy smile. Then all thoughts and doubts disappeared as she felt the rough skin of his hands slide up under her jumper.

Hands that knew hard work, not like Drew's almost feminine touch. The roughness of Andrew's fingers as they found their way inside her bra and over her nipples made her gasp and she arched against him, wrapping a leg over his to pull him closer. He lifted her jumper up to her neck, but it wasn't the cold air that made her shiver. He'd already dispersed with her bra and now his mouth was sucking one of her nipples, his hand holding it steady as his other hand was circling and tickling her other nipple.

'Fucking hell.' She bit her lips as he continued, his hand travelling down her stomach and into her jeans. She felt his fingers on her and almost exploded at his touch. But her jeans were too tight for his hand to be able to move much so he expertly undid the buttons, allowing himself freedom of movement. He reclaimed her mouth as she came, shuddering against him as she did.

'I love feeling you come,' he whispered against her ear.

'Trust me,' she said, breathless. 'The feeling is mutual,' he laughed. 'Your turn.' She pushed him onto his back and began unbuckling his belt. Screams of childish laughter rang out and he placed a hand on hers to stop her.

'Shall we carry this on tonight?' she nodded and moved away from him, fastening her buttons back up and putting her bra back on. 'I enjoy a bit of alfresco sex, but I've never been one for an audience.'

Chapter 24

The arrival of Carla and Kai dampened everyone's spirits that afternoon. Kai was a joy; he was wearing a pumpkin-embroidered jumper and jeans with what were unmistakably Timberland boots. Andi had never been able to afford anything other than replica ones so when she saw that Carla was dressed in an almost identical outfit and was accompanied by what appeared to be a professional photographer, she quickly surmised that she was after a photo opportunity. Kai giggled and smiled as Dennis and Kathy showed him around the farm. He delighted in the cows and was absolutely enthralled when Pumpkin tried to lick him.

Carla on the other hand moped most of the time and looked bored out of her brain except when the camera was pointed in her direction. Then she became a smiling and enthusiastic mum, scooping Kai up into the air and posing for the perfect photo amongst the pumpkins and Andi knew this would be plastered all over her social media as soon as she had hold of the files.

'Here's your jacket by the way.' Carla thrust it into Andi's hands as they were going, Dennis carrying what had become almost two hundred pounds worth of food, homemade wine and ten pumpkins. 'It's amazing what you find out about people when you least expect it.'

Andi had no idea what Carla meant by this and just smiled sweetly instead of thumping her which she was desperate to do. She knelt down to Kai. 'I hope you've enjoyed your visit to the Pumpkin Patch young man?'

'My boots got muddy.' He lifted one of his feet and there was the tiniest amount of dirt on the top.

'That's ok, it's just a little bit.' Andi brushed it off with her hand. 'Look, all clean.' The little boy threw his arms around her, and she hugged him back, slightly emotional by his show of affection and she wondered if he ever got any from Carla. Andi looked up at her, she was busy fishing her phone out of her bag as it was ringing.

'Oh hi, Andrew.' The hairs on the back of Andi's neck prickled. 'Yes, he's fine, he's had a great time. I can't wait to show you the photos.' She scooped Kai up and put the phone to his ear. 'Say hi to Daddy, Kai.'

'Hi, Daddy.' The little voice was full of excitement, but Andi didn't have a clue what he said next. Her whole world crumbled around her, and she fell backwards on to the floor.

'Andi?' Kathy's voice was full of concern and by her side instantly. 'Are you ok? You've gone all white. Andi?'

She didn't have a clue how long she'd been out for. All she remembered was talking to Kai about his muddy boot and then she just felt sick and faint, she knew her mum had been trying to talk to her, but she couldn't find the energy to answer and then she must have blacked out.

'Where am I?' Andi could feel something attached to her nose, there was a machine bleeping constantly and she could smell the unmistakable smell of hospital.

'Oh thank God!' It was her mum's voice. 'Dennis, she's awake.' Andi could see her mum peering over her and could feel her hand on hers, then her dad was there doing exactly the same. 'How are you feeling? You gave us quite a scare, the doctors haven't a clue what's going on.'

'I just fainted, Mum.' She felt groggy and incredible thirsty, and there was a shooting pain on the back of her head.

'You didn't faint, you collapsed.' Dennis rubbed her shoulder. 'Your mum said one minute you were fine, the next you were on the floor, mumbling. You've given yourself concussion from the bang to your head and went spark out. We had to call an ambulance; we couldn't get you to wake up.'

Andi tried to push herself up, she felt stiff and achy and needed to move. 'How long have I been out?'

'Nearly two days, it's just gone midnight on Thursday morning.' Her parents helped her scooch up the bed, Kathy plumping the pillow behind her head.

'I'd best ring Andrew and tell him.' Dennis patted her hand. 'He's been frantic you know, we had to force him to go home and try and get some sleep.'

Andi felt a surge of anger on hearing his name, but she didn't have a clue why. She racked her brain, but nothing was coming.

'Can I have some water please, Mum?' Kathy poured her a small glass.

'Sip it slowly,' she warned. 'Don't go guzzling it in case it makes you sick.

'I've told him.' Dennis was already back in the room. 'Says he's on his way.'

Andi felt better after the small drink and was desperately disappointed when her mum took the glass away and placed it out of her reach.

'Oh, Andi, thank God you're awake.' Andrew was by her bed, kissing her face, her hands, whatever he could find. 'I've been desperate.'

'How did you get here so quick?' Even her concussed brain could work out that it would take him more than a minute to get here from his house, but then she realised she didn't actually know where his house was.

'I was in the waiting room.' He looked sheepishly at Kathy and Dennis. 'I'm sorry, I know you told me to go home but I just couldn't. I wanted to be here when you woke up so one of the nurses took pity on me and let me stay.' He looked back to Andi and smoothed her hair. 'How are you feeling?'

'Like I've been hit by a truck.' She was feeling such an overwhelming mix of emotions that she couldn't make sense of it. On the one hand she was overjoyed to see him, but something was nagging at her.

'The doctors haven't got any idea why you blacked out.' He shook his head. 'I know you'd eaten because we'd had that picnic,' he smiled knowingly at her, and she felt a blush spreading across her cheeks. Oh yes, she could remember the picnic.

'You were fine all afternoon.' Kathy continued as they tried to piece together the events. 'We took Carla and Kai around…'

'Kai!' Andi sat up straight in the bed as if she'd been struck by a bolt of lightning. Her brain had suddenly filled in the gap of missing memory. Kai was Andrew's son. The anger that had been simmering away, began to bubble as if someone had turned the heat up. It wasn't anger that he had a son, she'd have been fine with that, it was anger that he hadn't told her, had blatantly lied to her face. 'Why didn't you tell me?' She turned to him, shouting angrily.

'Tell you what?' Andrew shot away from her in shock and surprise. 'Andi what's the matter?'

'You lied to me,' she screamed. 'Pretending to be Mr Nice Guy all the time when all this time you were keeping things from me.' He was looking at her with complete bafflement on his face.

'I don't know what I've done, Andi.' His voice was soft and pleading. 'Tell me what I've done.'

He went to grab her hand, but she snatched it away. 'You're worse than Drew.' His hand dropped by his side, and he stood up.

'I'll come back when you've calmed down.' He walked towards the door.

'Don't bother,' she shouted after him and watched as he walked slowly past the window with his head down.

'What on earth is all this noise about?' One of the nurses had appeared. 'You do know what time it is don't you? You've woken up half the ward,' she continued to scold. 'I'll have to ask you both to leave.' The last comment was directed towards her parents.

'Oh no, Nurse, I'm sorry, it wasn't them, it was me,' Andi begged whilst on the verge of tears. 'I promise, I'll be quiet.'

The nurse pursed her lips and Andi could see she was in two minds as to what to do. 'Well, I'm just glad to see you awake. I'll come back in five minutes to check you over and then your parents can go home and get some rest.'

'Whatever was all that about?' Kathy whispered and Andi finally let the tears flow.

'Kai is Andrew's son.' She could tell by the shocked looks on their faces that they had no idea.

'And he hadn't told you?' she shook her head.

'I wouldn't care if he had,' Andi sniffed. 'But he just out and out lied to me. Said Kai lived with his dad most of the time, saw Carla once or twice a year and he'd only met him a handful of times.'

'Why lie about it?' Dennis asked.

'He's just like all the rest isn't he.' She was so angry now. 'Just out for one thing and one thing only. I knew he was too good to be true.'

'I can't believe that of him, Andi.' She knew her mum was trying to be kind, to keep her calm but it wasn't working.

'At least I knew where I stood with Drew.' Kathy went to say something, but Dennis took her hand and shook his head at her.

'We'll head off home for a bit,' her dad spoke calmly. 'Chloe and Miley are looking after Pumpkin; they've got some news for you by the way but we'll let them tell you that.' They backed out of the door, blew her a kiss, and waved, leaving Andi alone with her thoughts.

Somehow, she managed to sleep again, probably her body doing what it needed to do. The doctor came in and explained that she had a low iron level which could account for the fainting and advised that she could go home later that afternoon. Her parents had dropped her in some toiletries and after assuring them that she was ok, they'd headed back to the shop and told her to let them know when she needed picking up.

Andi was desperate for a shower. She was now unhooked from all the machines so grabbed her towel, wash bag and clean clothes and headed into the bathroom once it was empty. She had the water as hot as she could stand and touched the lump on the back of her head gingerly as she washed her hair. She felt so much better now she was clean and back in her clothes rather than the hospital gown with the tie back that always left your knickers on show.

Perhaps she was being too harsh on Andrew, they still hardly knew each other after all, maybe she would give him a chance to explain at least. She bundled the things up and walked back to her room.

'Drew!' Of all the people she had expected to see sitting by her bed when she came back it wasn't him. 'What on earth are you doing here?'

'I've just heard.' He came straight over to her and took all the things out of her arms and went to take one of her hands.

'I'm not an invalid Drew.' What was it with men? She'd had just about enough of the lot of them.

'As soon as I found out I came straight here to see you.' Andi walked over to the window, grateful that she had a side room and wasn't on the main ward. 'I want you back Andi.'

'You want me what now?' She turned to find him down on one knee with a small black box in his hand.

'Will you marry me?' He popped open the box and inside was a diamond solitaire ring, just like the one Andi had seen a few months back when they'd gone to town. It had been in an antique shop, and she'd begged Drew to let her try it on. It had fitted to perfection, and she'd asked him to buy it but Drew being Drew, hadn't.

'Is that the one?' she asked, curiosity getting the better of her as she stepped closer. He nodded.

'I went back and got it for you.' So he wasn't all bad then, she thought to herself.

'I really don't know what to say.' Drew must have mistaken this for an acceptance because the next thing she knew he was standing up in front of her and kissing her. She pushed him away almost instantly but then realised too late that Andrew was standing at the door.

Chapter 25

The look on Andrew's face was one of sheer heartbreak and betrayal. He looked completely crushed as he walked away. Andi rushed after him, oblivious to Drew calling her and trying to wrench her arm free as he grabbed her on the way past.

'What are you doing?' She'd forgotten how much stronger he was than her and in her weakened state she couldn't get away.

'Let go of me, Drew.' She pulled at his fingers but somehow, he managed to now have hold of both her arms.

'Have you got another man already?' His eyes were bulging out of their sockets. 'I thought you were just winding me up the other day.'

'So what if I have?' She knew she was going to have to stand up to him using words rather than physical strength. 'At least I waited till we'd finished, unlike some.'

'Sapphire was a mistake.' He loosened his grip on her a little. 'It's taken me a while to realise it, Andi, but you're the best thing that ever happened to me and I want you to be my wife.'

There was a small part of her that considered this statement for the tiniest microsecond.

'Well then maybe you should have realised it sooner.' She broke free of his grasp. 'Goodbye Drew. I hope you won't take offence when I say that I never want to see you again, no, actually, I don't really care if you do take offence. It wasn't fun while it lasted, for the most part I was utterly miserable but too scared to tell you to leave.' She walked to the door. 'And one last thing.' She really felt like giving him a parting shot and knew exactly what she could say that would hurt him the most. 'You are absolutely shit in bed. I've had more orgasms this past week than you gave me in a year.' The look on his face was a picture and Andi didn't need a camera to capture it, she knew it would be frozen in her mind forever.

She didn't wait for him to reply, just rushed off down the corridor as fast as her legs and body would allow. There was no sign of Andrew outside the ward, so she quickly tried to get her bearings and realised she was on the fifth floor of the hospital. She'd just missed the lift and knew there was no way she could manage the stairs, so she stood and waited, angrily pushing the button in a vain attempt to make it go faster.

By the time she'd got to the entrance she was breathless and pinching her sides trying to alleviate the pain from the stitch that she'd given herself. She couldn't see him and there was no way she'd find him now. The hospital was one of the largest in the county. She had no idea where he'd parked or if he even had. For all she knew he could live just over the road or come on the bus. She walked back into the hospital and slowly made her way back to the ward, grateful to find that Drew had left.

She threw her things into the bag her parents had brought, not caring if she was mixing wet and dry clothes or dirty and clean. What on earth had gone so terribly wrong? She picked up her phone and rang Andrew but of course he didn't answer. She was just about to fire off a text message when the nurse came in with her discharge letter and said she could go home so she decided to try him again later and phoned her mum instead.

It was strange being back in her childhood room. It had been redecorated since she'd left but some of her teddy bears and ornaments were still out on the shelves. There was her school award for one hundred percent attendance and the witch figure she'd bought when they'd visited the small village of Burley in The New Forest. That had been one of her favourite holidays ever.

'Honestly you two make more noise trying to be quiet with all the shushing,' Andi said as she walked into the kitchen on the Friday morning to find her mum and dad making tea and toast. 'Hey Boy.' Pumpkin had rushed in from the garden at the sound of her voice and was currently on his hind legs, his front paws on her shoulders whilst he licked her face.

'He missed you,' Dennis remarked.

'I missed him too.' She ruffled the fur on his head and between his ears once he'd put all four paws back on the ground. She sat down at the breakfast bar and had a cup of tea and two slices of toast placed immediately in front of her. 'I could get used to this,' she said, biting into the crispy hot toast. 'You always did make the best toast, Dad.' She picked up her phone that she'd placed on the side and looked at the screen, no new notifications, so she put it straight back down.

Kathy and Dennis exchanged glances. 'Still nothing from Andrew?' Kathy asked and Andi shook her head. 'He'll come round; you did give him rather a good yelling at.'

'Don't remind me.' She put her head in her hands. The longer she'd had to think about it the more she'd come to realise that she may have slightly overreacted and should have at least given him a chance to explain instead of screaming at him in the middle of a hospital. So what if he had a son, most people their age did. She just wished he'd told her about it instead of lying to her. She didn't care if he came with baggage, she just wanted them to be together.

'Perhaps he'll come by the shop.' Her dad comforted her. 'You're coming in with us because the doctor said you're not to be left on your own, but you won't be doing any work until next week at least so it will be sitting behind the till in the shop or the barn and nothing else.'

'Oh, Dad, I'll be bored out my brains.' Andi hated just working the till, especially in the shop. If no one came in it was the most boring job in the whole place and with the barn open all this week, most people were going in there now.

'That's exactly the point,' he said, pointing his mug towards her. 'You've had a nasty bump on the head and far too much excitement. Your brain and body need a good rest.'

'Ok, Dad.' Andi knew better than to continue the argument with her dad. He had that look on his face which she'd seen hundreds of times over the years, and she knew it meant the discussion was at an end.

Half an hour later and she was in the back of her dad's car, with Pumpkin clipped in next to her on their way to The Pumpkin Patch. Andi's phone pinged and she couldn't stop the smile that spread across her face or the warm feeling that stole into her heart when she saw Andrew's name. Her dad must have seen it too for he caught her gaze in the wing mirror.

'Andrew?' he asked, and she nodded, desperate to open the message and read it but scared too in case it wasn't the words she was hoping for. 'It won't read any different if you open it now or this afternoon.'

Andi stared at her phone for a few seconds but knew that as usual her dad was right. Whatever the message said it wasn't going to change just because she didn't read it straight away. She took a deep breath and clicked on his name.

I think it's best if we don't see each other again.

'Well, that's that then.' She threw her phone to the side, startling poor Pumpkin who had been fast asleep. 'I've really fucked up this time.'

'It can't be that bad surely?' Kathy turned in her seat to face Andi. 'It's just a silly misunderstanding that's all, he'll understand.'

'He saw Drew kissing me in the hospital.' Andi hadn't told her parents this part yet.

'Drew was what?' Andi thought her dad was going to slam on the brakes, turn the car around and head off to Drew's flat. She'd never seen him so angry. 'I hope you gave him what for young lady. Who told him you were there anyway? Bloody nerve of the man.'

Andi explained what had happened, she told them about his proposal and the ring from the shop and then how he'd kissed her, and Andrew had seen it but by the time she'd got out of the hospital he was long gone.

'That ring was still in the shop last week when your dad and I walked past so that's total bollocks what Drew said.' Andi still found it odd when her mum swore. 'I remember you showing it me not long after you'd first seen it and I said it reminded me of your grandmother's engagement ring. I bet he went and bought it the other day and then just pretended so he could score some brownie points.'

'Well, he didn't score any brownie points. All that time I'd been waiting for him to ask me to marry him and then when he did, I knew I didn't want it.' She folded her arms across her chest. 'And that the man I do want had just borne witness to it and was walking right out of my life.'

'If it's meant to be, then it's meant to be.' Kathy had always been the pragmatic one. 'Just like me and your dad. I never thought we'd get back together but we did.' Andi couldn't help smiling at the loving look that crossed between her mum and dad.

'I'm never going to have what you two have.' She knew she was whining but she didn't care. She was fed up with her love life. She'd finally got rid of Drew and then something wonderful was on the horizon with Andrew but now that had gone too.

'You will,' Kathy insisted. 'Even if it's not with Andrew, there is someone out there waiting to love you and cherish you and for you to return the favour.'

'I hope you're right Mum.'

The day had been incredibly slow, just as Andi had predicted. Her bum ached from sitting on the stool behind the till. She'd served a grand total of three people who had purchased around fifty pounds worth of goods between them. She was grateful to see that the clock was nearing closing time and stepped off the stool and walked to the door with the sole purpose of switching the sign to closed. No one would know it was a little early.

'Are you open?' A man stood at the door just as she was about to lock it. He looked familiar to Andi, but she had no idea why. 'Is this the Pumpkin Patch?' His voice had a strong American accent, and she could see two other men with similar colouring and features to him standing behind.

No, it couldn't be them.

'Yes, this is The Pumpkin Patch.' She kept looking at them, absolute disbelief that this could be happening. Surely, they were just lookalikes, pranksters perhaps.

'From Tik Tok?' he pointed at his phone.

Andi nodded; her mouth suddenly dry. 'I can't believe it!' They were here, they were really here. 'It's you, it's actually you!'

Chapter 26

Andi was in shock. She never for one minute thought that her favourite group would be standing in the shop. She knew they were in the UK, had seen them on various shows promoting their new album but they were here in the shop and from what they were saying, they'd seen the Tik Tok video.

'It's so great to meet you.'

'We all loved the video.

'Can we meet Pumpkin?'

'I can't believe you're here.' She was all excitement and nerves. 'I'll go and get him.'

Andi fetched Pumpkin from the back, and he immediately jumped on them, reaching up to lick their faces.

'He's so cute.'

Three men dressed in black appeared at the door and informed the group that it was time to go.

'Can I go and fetch the others?' Andi knew they would want to meet them too.

'We have to go.' The tallest one took out his phone and handed it to a bodyguard. 'On our way to the next gig but we'd love to do a quick video though?'

'Oh yes please.' Andi held Pumpkin and the group popped up from behind the counter just as they had done in their spoof version.

'We'll post it for you later.' They stroked Pumpkin's head and waved goodbye from the door.

'Was great to meet you.'

'Sorry we couldn't stay longer.'

'And you.' Andi watched them leave, disbelief at what had just happened. No one was going to believe her, damn, why hadn't she thought to take a photo of them on her own phone?

'Who was that in the black van?' Dennis was all concern as he came into the shop a few moments later.

'It was them!' Andi felt like she was in a daydream. Her dad looked at her with a blank expression. 'The group. You know, Waffle House?'

'I think you hit your head a bit harder than we thought,' Dennis laughed. 'Here Kathy? Guess who Andi thinks has just been in the shop?'

As predicted, none of them believed her and despite her protests to the contrary, with no proof she was unable to get them to believe her.

'Your mum told me Drew proposed,' Chloe said that evening as they sat in Andi's living room. Andi had been allowed home for the night as long as Chloe stayed with her, so they'd planned an evening of Zac Efron films starting with 17 again.

'Don't remind me,' Andi said. 'Oh I love this bit, where they're dancing.'

'Stop changing the subject.' Chloe pressed pause on the remote and turned to face her. 'What's been going on?' Andi reeled off the whole sorry story to Chloe and she felt utterly relieved when she was finally unburdened. 'Well that's a turn up for the books, isn't it? He got down on one knee and everything?'

'Right there in the hospital,' Andi nodded. 'He was only doing it because he thought I'd be daft enough to say yes, I know he doesn't love me, to be honest, I don't even care if he does, I'm just glad to be out of that relationship.'

'And what about Andrew?' Chloe asked hopefully. 'Surely you have some way of messaging him?'

'It's really bad, Chlo, but I don't even know his last name or the name of his business,' she put her head in her hands. 'I haven't got a clue where he lives, for all I know he could be some travelling gardener with a woman in every city from here to John O'Groats. He might not even be a gardener.' With this statement Andi remembered the callouses on his hands as they touched her skin and was convinced that at least this was probably true.

'I hate to admit it, Andi,' Chloe looked at her with a solemn and serious expression. 'But you're a slut.' Andi smacked her playfully on the arm. 'Only joking. You must know something about him or somewhere he goes? Didn't you say you had lunch with him somewhere?'

'Books and Brews!' Andi almost shouted it out with glee. 'I could leave a message with Claire and Harry. I'm sure he said he went there quite a bit.'

'Eh Voila!' Chloe flourished her hands and bowed her head. 'No need to thank me, just make sure I'm chief bridesmaid at the wedding,' she paused. 'Speaking of which?'

Andi looked at her friend through narrowed eyes. 'Speaking of which, what?'

'Will you be my chief bridesmaid?' Chloe flashed her left hand at Andi to show a beautiful emerald ring.

'Oh My God!' Andi screamed with delight, Chloe screamed with delight and somehow, they hugged each other and started jumping around the room, much to the annoyance of Pumpkin, who had been quite happily asleep on Chloe's feet. 'You're getting married! Tell me everything.'

'So, you know how I thought Miley was keeping something from me, turns out she was. She'd been planning this huge proposal night for us. That's why she kept popping home at random times and always seemed to be around.' They sat back down on the sofa. 'She arranged a string quartet to play at this posh restaurant in Oxford and then pulled two rings out after dessert and asked me to marry her. I said yes, obviously.'

Andi could see the sheer delight on her friend's face. 'This calls for champagne.' She headed into the kitchen and came back with a bottle of Echo Falls. 'This will have to do.' Andi poured the wine into two tumblers. 'So are you ok about the oral sex now? Did you speak to her about it?'

'I did,' Chloe admitted. 'I put my big girl pants on well, I didn't actually have any on at the time.' Andi shook her head in disbelief. 'She was literally doing the deed when I just came out with it.'

'Fucking hell, Chlo, talk about passion killer.' Andi almost spat her wine out.

'I know, I know. But I was just lying there thinking oh for fuck's sake hurry up already and she was licking and sucking, and it just wasn't happening, so I just said, we need to talk.' Andi was in shock.

'There's you getting too much and me not getting enough,' she remarked.

'She took it really well actually and now we are planning on spicing up our sex life.' Chloe pulled out her phone and showed Andi a photo. 'We're going to get some of these.'

'TMI!' Andi averted her gaze from the array of sex toys on the screen, then looked back quickly. 'What the hell is that?' She pointed to something that resembled a penis with what looked like another penis growing out of the opposite end.

'Oh that's a double ender. We can both use it at the same time and then our cli…'

Andi placed a hand over Chloe's mouth. 'There are some things that even a best friend doesn't need to know.'

'Perhaps you're right.' She pressed play back on the remote control. 'So what's the plan of action for getting Andrew back then?'

Chloe dropped Andi and Pumpkin at Books and Brews on her way to work. She'd already written a short note for Andrew because the likelihood of him actually being there was little to none. Claire greeted her warmly as she explained that she was looking for Andrew.

'You've just missed him.' Disappointment washed over Andi. 'Honestly, about ten minutes ago he popped in for his normal tea and cake takeaway.'

'Can I leave this with you then?' Claire nodded and took the envelope from her.

'Tell me if it's not my place, but he looked awful miserable.' Andi hoped this meant he was missing her. 'And I'm sure Harry said there was a woman with him, she was shouting and hooraying at him something terrible. I'd just nipped to the loo, so I didn't see her, Harry said she stormed out when she didn't get the answer she wanted from him.'

'Thanks, Claire.' Andi wasn't sure if this was good or bad news. 'You'd best pack me up a few bacon butties, it's Halloween tomorrow and I'm sure it's going to be very busy,' she smiled. 'Plus, Dad is picking me up in ten minutes and I had to bribe him for the lift.'

Andi's premonition of the day proved to be true and despite her dad insisting she wasn't to do any heavy work; it was unavoidable, and all hands were needed around the field and the barn. They closed the shop at midday as no one had been in there and it meant they could focus on all the activities.

Pumpkin was in constant demand but after two hours even his patience had run out and Andi put him in the back of the shop with a chew where he could chill out for a bit. She longed to join him. The bacon butties had been the only thing any of them had had to eat that day. There hadn't been time for breaks and Andi made the decision to order in some sandwiches and hot drinks for them all.

Luckily, it didn't take long to arrive, and she put the rather large bag of goodies and the trays of hot drinks onto one of the flatbed trollies and wheeled it into the barn. She was greeted with happy faces and relieved smiles as one by one the staff of The Pumpkin Patch found a spare minute to grab a sausage roll and a cup of pumpkin spiced latte.

'Blimey, I needed that,' Fran said, popping the rubbish in the bin and the cardboard cup in the recycling pile. 'We'll soon be out of pumpkins at this rate.'

'I honestly can't believe it's taken off so well. I just hope the parties are as popular tomorrow,' Kathy remarked. 'I know we've sold all the tickets, but people still need to come, and we still need to make sure they all have a good time, or they'll be asking for refunds.'

'It will be fine, Mum.' Andi placed a reassuring hand on her shoulder. 'You wait and see.'

'Do we all know what we're wearing?' Preeti butted in. 'I've splashed out and bought myself a sexy witch outfit. I can dumb it down for the kiddie party with a cloak and then you just wait for the evening. I thought Owen's eyes were going to pop out when I showed him. He wants me to keep it on when I get home tomorrow evening.' She laughed naughtily and then headed off to serve a group of teenagers that had been out to pick their pumpkins and now wanted to pay.

'You wait and see what me and your dad are coming as,' Kathy smiled mischievously. 'It was his idea, it's just brilliant.' Kathy was then called away, followed swiftly by Fran and Andi's attention was soon taken up with the craft table. Thankfully, she already had a dress from a Bridgerton inspired ball she had gone to last year with Chloe and she'd adapted it to make it more appropriate for Halloween. She couldn't wait to wear it again.

She loved the Regency era; the empire line dress flattered her figure because it flowed out from her bust. It was black and silver and she'd bought a masquerade mask to wear with it and had added a cloak with flowing sleeves and high collar to complete the vampire look. She was absolutely determined to enjoy herself tomorrow. There were a few more things to sort out after closing this evening, but she had decided that tomorrow was going to be the start of her new life and if Andrew wasn't to be a part of that, then so be it. She just needed to get her heart to agree with her head.

Chapter 27

Halloween morning dawned bright and clear and oh so very cold. There was a thick frost on the ground and Andi was thankful that they had spent the extra time last night bringing in the last of the pumpkins from the field and into the relative warmth of the barn. If they hadn't, most of them would have been ruined.

She watched the sunrise with her parents, Lewis and Pumpkin. They sat on one of the benches that overlooked the farm, drinking hot chocolate and munching on gingerbread biscuits. The four of them had already been up since five so even though it was only eight, it felt like elevenses to them.

'I'm so glad we decided to do this,' Kathy said, breaking the silence.

'Do what?' Lewis asked.

'Buy this place and work it as a family,' Dennis scoffed at her words.

'I seem to remember you all thought it was a terrible idea and that I must have completely and utterly lost my marbles,' Kathy laughed.

'Ah yes but look how wonderful it turned out in the end.' He placed an arm around his wife's shoulders and hugged her to him. Andi swallowed hard and tried not to think about Andrew. Today was a new beginning, a fresh start. It was All

Hallows Eve, the night when the sprits of the dead walked the earth, and she intended treating it like New Year's Eve and putting the past year behind her.

'I'm so glad we're not opening early today. I think we'll all need a holiday once Halloween is over.' Andi looked at her parents, who hadn't heard a word she'd just said and were just holding hands and staring out into the sky. She would consider herself very lucky indeed if she found someone that looked at her that way after forty years of marriage. As if they'd fetch you the moon and the stars if it would make you happy.

'Good job we're closed tomorrow then, isn't it?' Lewis exchanged a glance with Andi after looking at his parents. 'It is kind of sweet though.' Andi nodded in agreement and rested her head on his shoulder, content to just be.

Andi couldn't believe how many people had turned up for the party without even having a ticket. She couldn't understand the sudden interest and why everyone wanted to take photos with Pumpkin, who was not playing ball at all and being decidedly grumpy in the knitted pumpkin hat Preeti had made for the occasion. He'd only kept it on for five minutes before pawing at it and pulling it off and despite her best efforts, he was not having it back on. He might be soft and amicable most of the time, but he could also be stubborn and getting a husky to do something they didn't want to do was nigh on impossible.

They had to turn people away and shut the gate in the end, but then they noticed that lots of teenage girls were still jumping over it and standing outside the shop taking selfies. Andi decided there was nothing for it but to ask.

'Erm, girls.' She approached a small group. 'What's the fascination all of a sudden?'

'Oh my God!' One of them screamed and then the others did. 'It's you! Can I take a picture? Were they lovely? Did you speak with them?'

'With whom?' Andi was baffled.

'With the boys, of course.' Light dawned on Andi, but she couldn't work out how they knew they'd been there. 'Look.' She flicked through her phone and showed Andi a TikTok video where the group had stitched the video of their visit with the original Pumpkin Patch video. Well, at least everyone would believe her now. She still couldn't believe how excited the girls were getting. They weren't even there anymore.

'They were all very lovely but only here for a few minutes,' Andi said in the hope that this would get them to leave.

'Can we go in the shop?' one asked.

'We want to see Pumpkin,' another exclaimed.

'I'm sorry girls, but the shop is closed today, and Pumpkin is going home.' She suddenly decided that the best place for the now famous husky was anywhere but here and had asked Fran to come and get him for a few hours. There were disappointed sighs and despondent looks on their faces, but after more selfies and group photos, the teenage girls must have got bored and headed home. She hoped that this was it for the day, they weren't going to be able to deal with hordes of teenagers outside whilst trying to have a party inside.

The children's party had gone off without a hitch and everyone seemed to have had a great time. Fran had brought Matthew in for the party who was dressed as an extremely cute werewolf, complete with furry hands, which he refused to keep on for any length of time because apparently, they made his hands itchy. Pumpkin was back on form after his time away and posed time and again for photos with the children, but he was still refusing his pumpkin hat.

Kathy and Dennis were The Mad Hatter and Queen of Hearts from Alice in Wonderland. Andi couldn't believe the amount of work that must have gone into their costumes, and they had somehow become an unexpected attraction for the party.

They played old-fashioned party games with a Halloween twist, like pin the tail on the werewolf, pass the zombie parcel and musical pumpkins. The children squealed with delight when they were all handed goodie bags at the end of the party filled with jelly snakes, sugar mice and chocolate eyeballs. Andi, Chloe, and Fran had spent many hours sourcing sweets that would be suitable for all, and each bag was carefully labelled with any allergens or dietary needs.

It was with a huge sigh of relief that they waved goodbye to the last family before slumping down on to the hay bales and groaning.

'Do you realise we only have three hours until people start arriving again?' Lewis remarked, his green face paint now all over his Frankenstein jacket rather than his face after three rather exuberant six-year-olds had spilt their drinks all over him.

'You wouldn't think a few kids could make all this mess,' Preeti exclaimed.

'A few kids, Preeti?' Andi looked at the decimated barn. 'There was almost two hundred people in here and now we've got to get it clean and redressed for this evening.'

'Well, what on earth are you all waiting for then?' They all turned to find Chloe and Miley standing in the door dressed as Batman and Robin. 'The cavalry has arrived.'

With music to sing and dance along to, the time and chores passed quickly and easily and with twenty minutes to spare, the barn had been transformed into a Halloween dream. Dennis had had a brilliant idea a few weeks ago to collect and dry as many leaves as they could find, which wasn't hard considering the amount of trees that surrounded the shop and farm. These leaves were now strewn over the floor to create a crunchy autumnal carpet.

Solar powered pumpkin lanterns that had been hanging outside all day to charge were now hung from every rafter. Countless carved pumpkins with battery powered flickering candles were positioned on virtually every surface. Andi had wanted to use real candles but because of the amount of dry straw and people, Kathy had advised against it due to the fire risk. Naked flames and a barn full of what was basically kindling, were not a good mix.

Ben, One of Lewis' friends, had offered to act as DJ.

'Where's all your equipment?' Dennis asked as Ben arrived with just a few speakers.

'Here,' he showed Dennis the boxes.

'But where are the decks and all your records?' Andi could see that her dad was confused. 'How are you going to play music without it?'

'You have heard of downloads and streaming, haven't you, Mr Wilson.' Ben had been friends with Lewis since senior school, so he was allowed to tease.

'Of course.' Dennis puffed up his chest. 'I have got an iTunes account; I'll have you know.'

'All you need these days is one of these,' he pulled out his phone. 'And a few speakers. I have lights too, but Lewis said you didn't need them.'

Once Ben had set up, he played a song and Dennis was so impressed that he smacked him proudly on the back as if he'd just invented the wheel or something.

'Quickly,' Chloe shouted. 'It's almost time.' There was a brief panic as everyone took their respective places to welcome their guests for the evening. They'd made an executive decision between them to use some of the ticket money to hire the local fish and chip van to serve the food and drink so they could mingle and enjoy the evening themselves. After the busiest week at The Pumpkin Patch ever, they were all looking forward to letting their hair down. Matthew was staying the night with Fran's parents, so everyone was here, dressed up and ready for a good time.

Although they had stated that masks were optional, most people wore them, and they varied from full face coverings to tiny eye masks and from Halloween themes to pretty butterflies. Within thirty minutes, the barn was comfortably full, and the party was in full swing. Ben put Thriller on and with screams of delight, Andi, Lewis, and Chloe flew to the dance floor and started dancing just like Michael Jackson. Others tried to join in, some already masters like them and some not caring at all and just enjoying themselves.

They carried on for a few more songs until breathless from dancing and laughing and feeling incredibly hot because she'd forgotten how tight the bodice was across the bust, Andi walked towards the barn door, intent on grabbing a drink and a breath of fresh air.

She almost crashed into the man who was standing in her way. He was tall and dressed as a Regency gentleman, except his clothes were tattered and torn and his make-up and mask made him the perfect zombie. Andi could see his mouth moving and assumed he was talking to her, but she couldn't hear over the music and chatter.

'What did you say?' she shouted, cupping her ear with her hand in case he couldn't hear her either.

He spoke again and mimed dancing. Why not? She thought to herself. She was a free agent, and it was a dance after all, so she nodded and allowed him to lead her to the dance floor. He wore gloves as she did, but there was something familiar about the way her hand fitted inside his.

'Let's slow things down so we can all catch our breath,' Ben's voice came over the speakers. 'Here's Love Song for a Vampire.'

As the opening words started about coming into her arms again, Andi stepped into the open arms of the man and felt like she had come home. The feel of his chest was familiar, his aftershave was unmistakable, and she knew without a shadow of a doubt that it was Andrew. She knew that he knew it was her, her costume wasn't designed to mask her identity and her heart swelled to think he had come and sought her out on purpose.

She snuggled into his arms, content to just dance with him, talking could wait. She just wanted to enjoy being back in his embrace and, as she felt him place a soft kiss on the top of her head, she knew he felt the same.

Chapter 28

The song had ended but Andi didn't notice; she was too wrapped up in the feel of Andrew's arms around her back, the smell of his aftershave in her nose and the beat of his heart underneath her hand where she'd placed it on his chest, her other one was around his waist. They continued to sway and move slowly, their feet hidden under the carpet of leaves. It wasn't until someone bashed into them whilst doing a zombie hand jive that they stopped dancing and looked into each other's eyes.

'Shall we get a drink and go outside?' Andrew whispered in her ear, the sound of his voice sending shivers down her spine.

'I'd like that,' she nodded, not trusting her voice for more than a simple sentence.

They grabbed two glasses of punch from the table and in doing so Andi avoided her mum's eyes from across the barn and walked outside. It was already cold, and a frost was creeping over the ground, but this meant that the sky was clear with twinkling stars and a moon to light their way. A small group of teenage girls giggled and ran away as they approached the shop.

'What was that about?' Andrew asked.

'We had visitors the other day.' She explained to him about the group's visit and how they'd then posted photos on Tik Tok.

'It worked then.' He was smiling. 'It took a while, but it actually worked. The power of social media, eh?'

'We'll have to do a Christmas one next and see if we can get Cliff Richard to pop in,' she laughed. 'Mum and Preeti would go crazy if that happened.'

'Anything is possible,' he said, and she knew he wasn't just talking about the shop. They walked a little way, their hands millimetres away from each other but never touching. 'Listen.' He stopped and turned suddenly, taking both of her hands in his. 'I need to apologise.'

She shook her head. 'It's me that should be apologising. I didn't give you a chance to explain about Kai. I just barged in like a bull in a china shop, no thought for your feelings. I don't care that you have a son, it really doesn't matter, and I should have just let you tell me when the time was right.'

'Hang on a minute.' She looked at the bemused expression on his face. 'You think Kai is my son? Why would you think that?'

'When Carla was here last week, she rang you and got Kai to speak to you and he called you Daddy.' Andi didn't know why he was continuing to deny it, he'd had every opportunity now to admit it, she'd told him it didn't matter so why not just tell her.

'Carla never rang me,' he stated. 'I hadn't seen her until this morning when she gave me this.' He took out a piece of paper from his pocket, but Andi couldn't work out what it was. 'How do you know she was talking to me?'

'Because she called you Andrew.' Let him get out of that one she thought.

'Andrew IS Kai's dad.' He was laughing, but Andi really couldn't see the funny side of it at all.

'If you're not going to be serious, I'm going back to the party.' He took hold of her arm as she flounced off and pulled her back towards him.

'I'm not Andrew.' He was still laughing.

'You're just being absurd now.' Andi was getting angrier by the second. 'Of course you're Andrew, it's what everyone calls you.'

'Carla doesn't.' Andi looked at him. 'Carla calls me Drew because her ex is Andrew.' She still wasn't convinced. 'Remember when we first met?' How could she forget? The sight of him in wet britches and shirt was imprinted on her mind forever. 'When I said to call me Drew.'

'There is no way she's been with two people called Andrew.' Andi was having a hard time believing this. 'There aren't that many Andys in Pickle Grove.'

'You're called Andi,' he stated. 'And your boyfriend is called Andrew too.'

'I see your point.' A small flame of hope flickered inside her heart. 'So, Kai isn't your son?' He shook his head. 'And you are definitely broken up with Carla?'

He nodded and handed her the piece of paper. 'She came to show me this, it had the opposite effect to what she thought.'

'I'd forgotten about this.' She unfolded the paper and reread her own writing. 'The Pumpkin Pact. But how did she get hold of it?' Andrew shrugged his shoulders. 'My jacket! Mum gave her my jacket when she got wet from the tap, she must have found it in one of the pockets.'

'When I read it, it reminded me of that time when we were planning to make Carla and Drew jealous, and I remembered how miserable I was with her and how unhappy you were.' He was looking at her with such an endearing smile on his face that she was about to melt into a heap of mush. 'She wanted us to get back together, she thought showing me what you'd written would make me think you were just a silly girl, but it made me see how mean and nasty she was and just how wonderful you were. She really wasn't very happy when I told her it was over once and for all.'

'Does she call her ex, Andrew?' There was just one little thing bugging her still.

'No, Andy.' His face switched to confused again. 'Why?'

'Because in this…' she waved the plan at him. 'I call you Andrew, so I bet the spiteful cow purposefully called Kai's dad Andrew or she didn't even phone him at all and just pretended. I don't really remember much after that bit.'

'Talking about that.' Andi knew they were going to have to at some point. 'In the hospital, when you kissed Drew.'

'I didn't kiss him,' she interrupted. 'He kissed me, and I slapped him and came after you, but I couldn't find you. I'd never felt so desperate in my entire life.'

'I know.' He cupped her face with his hands and lifted her lips to his. It was the softest and sweetest kiss she'd ever had, and it made every inch of her tingle from the top of her head to the tip of her toes. 'Chloe found my business on Facebook and messaged me. I should have known though; I should have trusted you.'

'It doesn't matter now.' She took his hands into hers and held them over her heart. 'Let's make a new plan, together.'

He nodded eagerly. 'I promise to love you every day.' Her head snapped up at his words. 'Because I do love you. I love you with every fibre of my being, with every beat of my heart and with every breath in my lungs.'

'I love you too.' She really didn't know what else to say. 'I promise to share my thoughts and feelings with you.'

'I promise to talk to you about anything that's bothering me.' They continued with their pledges, each taking it in turn to say something and then the other agreeing and nodding until finally Andi really had nothing else left to say except...

'I promise to kiss you good morning and good night and every time that I see you and all the time in between,' he smiled and pulled her lovingly into his arms.

'I promise the same.' And with that, The Pumpkin Pact was sealed with a kiss.

THE END

A Little Note

I started writing this in September 2022 after a very hot summer here in the UK, it had been a stressful time for my family. It's now August 2023 and the year didn't get any better. I lost my wonderful godfather earlier in the year and my beloved and only uncle last week, which has hit the family hard.

It's times like these that make me so very thankful for my family and friends.

My mother remains the strongest woman I know, I don't think anyone will ever beat her to that title.

I wouldn't be able to get up most days without the love and laughter that my dearest friends give me, they build me back up when I need it most.

Being a mother is the hardest job you will ever have but I wouldn't change it for the world. My children are almost grown up now and I am so incredibly proud of them both.

Writing is quite a solitary business, but I have met so many wonderful people along the way. They know who they are and I will be forever grateful for their support.

Special thanks as always to Kim who puts up with my constant book ideas and covers being sent to her at random times of the day and night.

And a heartfelt thank you to you, the reader, I hope that you enjoyed The Pumpkin Pact and that it made you feel snuggly and warm on a cool autumn day.

Until next time.

Charlie xx

About the Author

I was born in Coventry but now live in Nuneaton. I married the love of my life nearly 25 years ago and we have two almost grown-up children. We share our lives with two mad dogs as well.

Writing is a great passion of mine. I love creating stories and characters, they help me escape from the world for a while and I hope readers feel the same.

I am a huge fan of All Creatures Great and Small, Call the Midwife and Bridgerton. I love history and romance.

I also write under Florence Keeling and for children as Lily Mae Walters.

Coming Soon

A Cranberry for Christmas, publishing on 17th October 2023.

Thank you for choosing this book. If you enjoyed it, please consider telling your friends or leaving a review on Goodreads or the site where you bought it. Word of mouth is an author's best friend and much appreciated.

Also by Charlie Dean

I Love You, Always, Forever

By Florence Keeling

A Little in Love

The Word is Love

Please Remember Me

Love, Lies and Family Ties

By Lily Mae Walters

Josie James and The Teardrops of Summer

Josie James and The Velvet Knight

Brittle's Academy for The Magically Unstable

Follow me on Twitter

@CharlieADean

@KeelingFlorence

@LilyMaeWalters1

Printed in Great Britain
by Amazon